SACRAMENTO STATE COLLEGE LIBRARY

This book is due on the last date stamped below.

Failure to return books on the date due will result in assessment of prescribed fines.

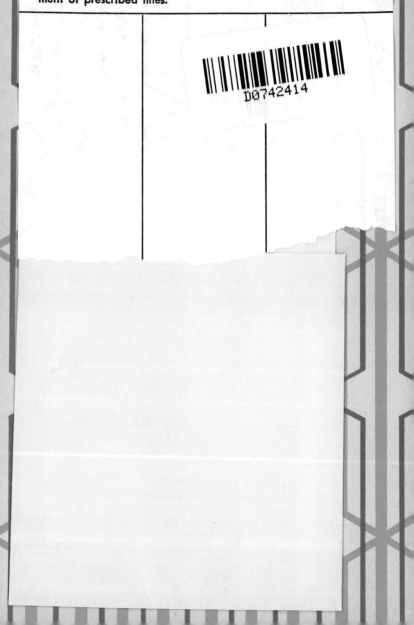

D0742414

THE
UNCLE OF AN ANGEL

"When Miss Lee and Mr. Brown regularly went down to the rocks."

[See page 60.

THE
UNCLE OF AN ANGEL

AND OTHER STORIES

BY

THOMAS ALLIBONE JANVIER

ILLUSTRATED

Short Story Index Reprint Series

BOOKS FOR LIBRARIES PRESS
FREEPORT, NEW YORK

First Published 1891
Reprinted 1969

STANDARD BOOK NUMBER:
8369-3152-1

LIBRARY OF CONGRESS CATALOG CARD NUMBER:
73-98578

PRINTED IN THE UNITED STATES OF AMERICA

TO

C. A. J.

CONTENTS.

ILLUSTRATIONS.

THE UNCLE OF AN ANGEL.

I.

WHEN Mr. Hutchinson Port, a single gentleman who admitted that he was forty-seven years old and who actually was rising sixty, of strongly fixed personal habits, and with the most positive opinions upon every conceivable subject, came to know that by the death of his widowed sister he had been placed in the position of guardian of that sister's only daughter, Dorothy, his promptly formed and tersely expressed conception of the situation was that the agency by which it had been brought about was distinctively diabolical. The fact may be added that during the subsequent brief term of his guardianship Mr. Port found no more reason for

reversing this hastily formed opinion than did the
late King David for reversing his hastily expressed
views in regard to the general tendency of mankind
towards untruthfulness.

The two redeeming features of Mr. Port's trying
situation were that his duties as a guardian did not
begin at all until his very unnecessary ward was
nearly nineteen years old ; and did not begin active-
ly—his ward having elected to remain in France
for a season, under the mild direction of the elderly
cousin who had been her mother's travelling companion—until she was almost twenty. When she
was one-and-twenty, as Mr. Port reflected with much
satisfaction, he would be rid of her.

Neither by nature nor by education had Mr.
Hutchinson Port been fitted to discharge the duties
which thus were thrust upon him. His disposition
was introspective—but less in a philosophical sense
than a physiological, for the central point of his in-
trospection was his liver. That he made something
of a fetich of this organ will not appear surprising
when the fact is stated that Mr. Port was a Philadelphian. In that city of eminent good cheer livers
are developed to a degree that only Strasburg can
emulate.

Naturally, Mr. Port's views of life were bounded,
more or less, by what he could eat with impunity;
yet beyond this somewhat contracted region his
thoughts strayed pleasantly afield into the far wider
region of the things which he could not eat with
impunity ; but which, with a truly Spartan epicure-

anism, he did eat—and bravely accepted the bilious consequences! The slightly anxious, yet determined, expression that would appear upon Mr. Port's clean-shaven, ruddy countenance as he settled himself to the discussion of an especially good and especially dangerous dinner betrayed heroic possibilities in his nature which, being otherwise directed, would have won for him glory upon the martial field.

In minor matters—that is to say, in all relations of life not pertaining to eating—Mr. Port was very much what was to be expected of him from his birth and from his environment. Every Sunday, with an exemplary piety, he sat solitary in the great square pew in St. Peter's which had been occupied by successive generations of Ports ever since the year 1761, when the existing church was completed. Every other day of the week, from his late breakfast-time for some hours onward, he sat at his own particular window of the Philadelphia Club and contemplated disparagingly the outside world over the top of his magazine or newspaper. At four, precisely, for his liver's sake, he rode in the Park; and for so stout a gentleman Mr. Port was an excellent horseman. On rare occasions he dined at his club. Usually, he dined out; for while generally regarded as a very disagreeable person at dinners—because of his habit of finding fault with his food on the dual ground of hygiene and quality—he was in social demand because his presence at a dinner was a sure indication that the giver of it had a good culinary reputation; and in Philadelphia such a reputation is most highly prized. An irrelevant New York person, after meeting Mr. Port at several of the serious dinner-parties peculiar to Philadelphia, had described him as the animated skeleton; and had supplemented this discourteous remark with the still more discourteous observation that as a feature of a feast the Egyptian article was to be preferred—because it did not overeat itself, and did keep its mouth shut. However, Mr. Port's obvious rotundity destroyed what little point was to be found in this meagre witticism; and, if it had not, the fact is well-known in Philadelphia that New Yorkers, being descended not from an honorable Quaker ancestry but from successful operations in Wall Street, are not to be held accountable for their unfortunate but unavoidable manifestations of a frivolity at once inelegant and indecorous.

In regard to his summers, Mr. Port—after a month spent for the good of his liver in taking the waters at the White Sulphur—of course went to Narragansett Pier. It may be accepted as an incontrovertible truth that a Philadelphian of a certain class who missed coming to the Pier for August would refuse to believe, for that year at least, in the alternation of the four seasons; while an enforced absence from that damply delightful watering-place for two successive summers very probably would lead to a rejection of the entire Copernican system.

"And for so stout a gentleman Mr. Port was an excellent horseman."

II.

Being well advanced in years, well settled in habits
of a very rigid sort, and well provided with a highly choleric temperament, Mr. Hutchinson Port obviously was not the sort of person whom any intelligent ward would have selected for a guardian. And
equally true is it that Miss Dorothy Lee, thus thrust
by Fate into his by no means out-stretched arms,
was far from being the sort of young woman whom
even an uncle with strongly developed guardianly
instincts would have selected to practise upon as a
ward. There was a certain squareness about Dorothy's admirably dimpled chin that suggested forcibly (at least to a person cool enough not to be affected by the dimples) a temperament strongly in-
clining towards the positive ; and it was a matter
of record that when an argument arose as to the
propriety of gratifying some desire lying close to
Dorothy's heart, her singularly fine gray eyes, especially if the argument seemed to be going against
her, would be lighted up by a resolute glitter quite
startling to contemplate. In point of fact, argu-
ments of this nature had not arisen often ; for the
late Mrs. Lee had been a peace-at-any-price sort of
person, and for several years preceding her departure for another and a better world had suffered her

maternal prerogatives to remain entirely in abey-
ance.

"Poor dear mamma and I did not have a harsh
word for years, Uncle Hutchinson," Miss Lee explained, in the course of the somewhat animated
discussion that arose in consequence of Mr. Port's
declaration that a part of their summer would be
passed, in accordance with his usual custom, at the
White Sulphur, and of Dorothy's declaration that
she did not want to go there. This, her first summer in America, was the third summer after Mrs.
Lee's translation ; and since Dorothy had come into
colors again she naturally wanted to make the most
of them. "No, not a single harsh word did we ever
have. We always agreed perfectly, you know ; or
if mamma thought differently at first she always
ended by seeing that my view of the matter was
the right one. The only serious difference that I
remember since I was quite a little girl was that last
autumn in Paris ; when I had everything so perfectly arranged for a delightful winter in St. Petersburg,
and when mamma was completely set in her own
mind that we must go to the south of France. Her
cough was getting very bad then, you know, and
she said that a winter in Russia certainly would kill
her. I don't think it would have killed her, at least
not especially ; but the doctor backed mamma up—
and said some horrid things to me in his polite
French way—and declared that St. Petersburg was
not even to be thought of.

"And so, when I found that they were both

against me that way, of course I sacrificed my own feelings and told mamma that I would do just what she wanted. And mamma cried and kissed me, and said that I was an angel : wasn't it sweet of her? To be sure, though, she was having her own way, and I wasn't ; and I think that I was an angel myself, for I did want to go to Russia dreadfully. After all, as things turned out, we might almost as well have gone ; for poor dear mamma, you know, died that winter anyway. But I'm glad I did what I could to please her, and that she called me an angel for doing it. Don't you think that I was one? And don't you feel, sir, that it is something of an honor to be an angel's uncle?

"Now suppose I kiss you right on your dear little bald spot, and that we make up our minds not to go to that horrid sulphur place at all. Everybody says that it is old-fashioned and stupid ; and that is not the kind of an American watering-place that I want to see, you know. It would have been all very well if we'd gone there while I was in mourning, and had to be proper and quiet and retired, and all that ; but I'm not in mourning any longer, Uncle Hutchinson —and you haven't said yet how you like this break- fast gown. Do you have to be told that white lace over pale-blue silk is very becoming to your angel niece, Uncle Hutchinson? And now you shall have your kiss, and then the matter will be settled." With which words Miss Lee — a somewhat bewil- dering but unquestionably delightful effect in blond and blue—fluttered up to her elderly relative, embraced him with a graceful energy, and bestowed upon his bald spot the promised kiss.

"But—but indeed, my dear," responded Mr. Port, when he had emerged from Miss Lee's enfolding arms, "you know that going to the White Sulphur is not a mere matter of pleasure with me; it is one of hygienic necessity.   You forget, Dorothy "—Mr. Port spoke with a most earnest seriousness—"you forget my liver."

"Now, Uncle Hutchinson, what is the use of talking about your liver that way?   Haven't you told me a great many times already that it is an hereditary liver, and that nothing you can do to it ever will make it go right?   And if it is bound to go wrong anyway, why can't you just try to forget all about it and have as pleasant a time as possible?   That's the doctrine that I always preached to poor dear mamma—she had an hereditary liver too, you know —and it's a very good one.

"Anyhow, I've heard mamma say countless times that Saratoga was a wonderfully good place for livers; now why can't we go there?   Mamma always said that Saratoga was simply delightful— horse-racing going on all the time, and lovely drives, and rowing on the lake, and dancing all night long, and all sorts of lovely things.   Let's go to Saratoga, Uncle Hutchinson!   Mamma said that the food there was delicious—and you know you always are grumbling about the food those sulphur people give you.

"But what really would be best of all for you,

" Now suppose I kiss you right on your dear little bald spot."

Uncle Hutchinson," Miss Lee continued, with increasing animation, "is Carlsbad. Yes, that's what you really want—and while you are drinking the horrid waters I can be having a nice time, you know. Then, when you have finished your course, we can take a run into Switzerland ; and after that, in the autumn, we might go over to Vienna—you will be delighted with the Vienna restaurants, and they do have such good white wines there. And then, from Vienna, we really can go on and have a winter in Russia. Just think how perfectly delightful it will be to drive about in sledges, all wrapped up in furs" —Mr. Port shuddered ; he detested cold weather— " and to go to the court balls, and even, perhaps, to be present the next time they assassinate the Czar ! Oh, what a good time we are going to have ! Do write at once, this very day, Uncle Hutchinson, to Carlsbad and engage our rooms."

To a person of Mr. Port's staid, deliberate temperament this rapid outlining of a year of foreign travel, and this prompt assumption that the outline was to be immediately filled in and made a reality, was upsetting. His mental processes were of the Philadelphia sort, and when Miss Lee had completed the sketch of her European project he still was engaged in consideration of her argument in favor of throwing over the White Sulphur for Saratoga. However, he had comprehended enough of her larger plan to perceive that by accepting Saratoga promptly he might be spared the necessity of combating a far more serious assault upon his peace of mind and

digestion.   Travel of any sort was loathsome to
Mr. Port, for it involved much hasty and inconsiderate eating.

"Very well," he said, but not cheerfully, for this
was the first time in a great many years that he had
not made and acted upon plans shaped wholly in his
own interest, "we will try Saratoga, since you so
especially desire it; but if the waters affect my
liver unfavorably we shall go to the White Sulphur
at once."

"What!   We are not to go to Carlsbad, then?
Oh, Uncle Hutchinson, I had set my heart upon it!
Don't, now don't be in a hurry to say positively that
we won't go.   Think how much good the waters
will do you, and think of what a lovely time you
can have when your course is over, and you can eat
just as much as you want of anything!"

But even by this blissful prospect Mr. Port was
not to be lured; and Dorothy, who combined a good
deal of the wisdom of the serpent with her presum-
able innocence of the dove, perceived that it was the
part of prudence not further to press for larger victory.

"And from Saratoga, of course, we shall go to
the Pier," said Mr. Port, but with a certain aggress-
iveness of tone that gave to his assertion the air of
a proposition in support of which argument might
be required.

"To Narragansett, you mean?   Oh, certainly.
From what several people have told me about Narragansett I think that it must be quite entertaining,

and I want to see it. And of course, Uncle Hutchinson, even if I didn't care about it at all, I should
go all the same ; for I want to fall in exactly with
your plans and put you to as little trouble as possible, you know. For if your angel wasn't willing to
be self-sacrificing, she really wouldn't be an angel
at all."

Pleasing though this statement of Early Christian
sentiment was, it struck Mr. Port—as he subsequently revolved it slowly in his slowly-moving mind—as
lacking a little on the side of practicality ; for Miss
Lée, so far, unquestionably had contrived to upset
with a fine equanimity every one of his plans that
was not absolutely identical with her own.

III.

On the whole, the Saratoga expedition was not a
success. Even on the journey, coming up by the
limited train, Miss Lee was not favorably impressed
by the appearance of her fellow-passengers. Nearly
all of the men in the car (most of whom immediately betook themselves to the bar-room, euphoniously
styled a buffet, at the head of the train) were of a
type that would have suggested to one accustomed
to American life that variety of it which is found
seated in the high places of the government of the
city of New York ; and the aggressively dressed and
too abundantly jewelled female companions of these

men, heavily built, heavy browed, with faces marked
in hard lines, and with aggressive eyes schooled to
look out upon the world with a necessarily emphatic
self-assertion, were of a type that, without special
knowledge of American ways, was entirely recog-
nizable.   Albeit Miss Lee, having spent much time
in the mixed society of various European watering-
places, was not by any means an unsophisticated
young person, and was not at all a squeamish one,
she was sensibly relieved by finding that the chair
next to hers was occupied by a silvery-haired old
lady of the most unquestionable respectability;
and her composure was further restored, presently,
by the return to his chair, on the other side of her,
of Mr. Port : who had betaken himself to what the
conductor had told him was the smoking-room, and
who, finding himself in a bar-room, surrounded by
a throng of hard-drinking, foul-mouthed men, had
sacrificed his much-loved cigar in order to free himself from such distinctly offensive surroundings.

At their hotel, and elsewhere, Miss Lee and her
uncle encountered many of their fellow-passengers
by the limited train, together with others of a like
sort which previous trains had brought thither; and
while, on the whole, these were about balanced by
a more desirable class of visitors, they were in such
force as to give to the life of the place a very positive tone.

At the end of a week Dorothy avowed herself
disappointed.   " I never did think much of poor
dear mamma's taste, you know, Uncle Hutchinson,"

she said, with her customary frankness, "and what she found to like in this place I'm sure I can't imagine. It's tawdry and it's vulgar; and as for its morals, I think that it's worse than Monte Carlo. I suppose that there is a nice side to it, for I do see a few nice people; but, somehow, they all seem to stand off from each other as though they were afraid here to take any chances at all with strangers. And I don't blame them, Uncle Hutchinson, for I feel just that way myself. What you ought to have done was to have hired a cottage, and then people would have taken the trouble to find out about us; and when they'd found that we were not all sorts of horrid things we should have got into the right set, and no doubt, at least if we'd stayed here through August, we should have had a very nice time.

"But we're not having a nice time, here at this noisy hotel, Uncle Hutchinson, where the band can't keep quiet for half an hour at a time, and where the only notion that people seem to have of amusement is to overdress themselves and wear diamonds to dinner and sit in crowds on the verandas and dance at night with any stranger who can get another stranger to introduce him and to drive over on fine afternoons to that place by the lake and drink mixed drinks until some of them actually get tipsy. I really think that it all is positively horrid. And so I'm quite willing now to go to the White Sulphur. It is stupid, I know, but I've always heard that it is intensely respectable. I will get my packing all done this afternoon, and we will start to-morrow

morning; and I think that you'd better go and telegraph for rooms right away."

But to Dorothy's surprise, and also to her chagrin,
Mr. Port refused to entertain her proposition. He
fully agreed with her in her derogatory estimate of
Saratoga life as found at Saratoga hotels; and he
cherished also a private grief incident to his (mistaken) belief that the cooking was not so good as
he remembered it, bright in the glamour of his sound
digestion in his youthful past. On the other hand,
however, the waters certainly were having a most
salutary effect upon his liver; and the move to
Virginia would involve spending two days of hot
weather in toilsome travel, sustained only by such
food as railway restaurants afford. Therefore Mr.
Port declared decidedly that until the end of July
they would remain where they were—and so gave
his niece the doubtful pleasure of an entirely new
experience by compelling her to do something that
she did not want to do at all. It was a comfort to
Mr. Port, in later years, to remember that he had
got ahead of Dorothy once, anyhow.

Being a very charming young person, Miss Lee
could not, of course, be grumpy; yet grumpiness
certainly would have been the proper word with
which to describe her mood during her last fortnight at Saratoga had she not possessed such extraordinarily fine gray eyes and such an admirably
dimpled chin. The fact must be admitted that she
contrived to make her uncle's life so much of a burden to him that his staying powers were strained

to the utmost. Indeed, he admitted to himself that he could not have held out against such tactics for another week; and he perceived that he had done injustice to his departed sister in thinking—as he certainly had thought, and even had expressed on more than one occasion in writing—that in permitting her European movements to be shaped in accordance with her daughter's fancies she had exhibited an inexcusable weakness.

It was a relief to Mr. Port's mind, and also to his digestion—for Dorothy's grumpiness produced an effect distinctly bilious—when the end of July arrived and his own and his charming ward's views once more were brought into harmony by the move to Narragansett Pier. Fortunately, while somewhat disposed to stand upon her own rights, Miss Lee was not a person who bore malice; a pleasing fact that became manifest on the moment that she began to pack her trunks.

"I am afraid, Uncle Hutchinson," she observed, on the morning that this important step towards departure was taken—"I am afraid that during the past week or so your angel may not have been quite as much of an angel as usual."

"No," replied Mr. Port, with a colloquial disregard of grammatical construction, and with perhaps unnecessary emphasis, "I don't think she has."

"But from this moment onward," Dorothy continued, courteously ignoring her uncle's not too courteous interpolation, and airily relegating into oblivion the recent past, "she expects to manifest

2

her angelic qualities to an extent that will make her appear unfit for earth. Very possibly she may even grow a pair of wings and fly quite away from you, sir—right up among the clouds, where the other angels are! And how would you like that, Uncle Hutchinson?"

In the sincere seclusion of his inner consciousness Mr. Port admitted the thought that if Dorothy had resolved herself into an angelic *vol-au-vent* (a simile that came naturally to his mind) at any time during the preceding fortnight he probably would have accepted the situation with a commendable equanimity. But what he actually said was that her departure in this aerated fashion would make him profoundly miserable. Mr. Port was a little astonished at himself when he was delivered of this gallant speech ; for gallant speeches, as he very well knew, were not at all in his line.

On the amicable basis thus established, Miss Lee and her guardian resumed their travels ; and, excepting only Mr. Port's personal misery incident to the alimentary exigencies of railway transportation, their journey from the central region of New York to the seaboard of Rhode Island was accomplished without misadventure.

IV.

In regard to Narragansett Pier, Miss Lee's opinions, the which she was neither slow in forming nor unduly cautious in expressing, at first were unfavorable.

"And so *this* is 'the Pier,' is it?" she observed in a tone by no means expressive of approval as she stood on the hotel veranda on the day of her arrival, and contemplated the rather limited prospect that was bounded at one end by the Casino and at the other by the coal-elevator. "If those smelly little stones out there are 'the Rocks' that people talk about at such a rate I must confess that I am disappointed in them"—Mr. Port hastened to assure her that the Rocks were in quite a different direction—"and if that is the Casino, while it seems a nice sort of a place, I really think that they might have managed the arch so as not to have that horrid green house showing under it. And what little poor affairs the hotels are! Really, Uncle Hutchinson, I don't see what there is in this little place to make such a fuss about."

"Dorothy," replied Mr. Port, with much solemnity, "you evidently forget—though I certainly have mentioned the fact to you repeatedly—that the climate of this portion of Rhode Island is the most distinctively antibilious climate to be found upon the whole coast of North America. For persons possessing delicate livers—"

"Oh, bother delicate livers—at least, I beg your pardon, Uncle Hutchinson," for an expression of such positive pain had come into Mr. Port's face at this irreverent reference to an organ that he regarded as sacred that even Dorothy was forced to make some sort of an apology. "Of course I don't want to bother your poor liver more than it is bothered anyway; but, you know, I haven't got a liver, and I don't care for climates a bit. What I mean is: what do people do here to have a good time?"

"In the morning," replied Mr. Port, "they bathe, and in the afternoon they drive to the Point. This morning we shall bathe, Dorothy—bathing is an admirable liver tonic—and this afternoon we shall drive to the Point."

"Good heavens! Is that all?" exclaimed Miss Lee. "Why, it's worse than Saratoga. Do you mean to say, Uncle Hutchinson, that people don't dance here, and don't go yachting, and don't have lunch-parties, and don't play tennis, and don't even have afternoon teas?"

"I believe that some of these things are done here," replied Mr. Port, in a tone that implied that such frivolities were quite beyond the lines of his own personal interests. "Yes," he continued, "I am sure that all of them are done here now—for the Pier is not what it used to be, Dorothy. The quiet air of intense respectability that characterized Nar-

ragansett when it was the resort only of a few of
the best families of Philadelphia has departed from
it—I fear forever! But, thank Heaven, its climatic
characteristics remain intact. When you are older,
Dorothy, and your liver asserts itself, you will appre-
ciate this incomparable climate at its proper value."

"Well, it hasn't asserted itself yet, you know ; and
I must say I'm devoutly thankful that something
has happened to wake up the quiet and intensely respectable Philadelphians before I had to come
here. But I'm very glad, dear Uncle Hutchinson,"
Miss Lee continued, winningly, "that this climate
is so good for you, and I'm sure I hope that you
won't have a single bilious attack all the time that
you are here. And you'll take your angel to the
dances, and to see the tennis, and you'll give her
lunch - parties, and you'll take her yachting, won't
you, you dear? But I know you will ; and if this
were not such a very conspicuous place, and might
make a scandal, I'd give you a very sweet kiss to pay
you in advance for all the trouble that you are going to take to make your angel enjoy herself. You
needn't bother about the teas, Uncle Hutchinson—
for the most part they're only women, and stupid."

Being still somewhat cast down by painful memories of that trying final fortnight in Saratoga, during which he and his niece had pulled so strongly
in opposite directions, Mr. Port heard with a lively
alarm this declaration of a plan of campaign which,
if carried out, would wreck hopelessly his own comfort of body and peace of mind. Obviously, this

was no time for faltering. If the catastrophe was to be averted, he must speak out at once and with a decisive energy.

"I need not tell you, Dorothy," he began, speaking in a most grave and earnest tone, "that it is my desire to discharge in the amplest and kindest manner my duties towards you as a guardian—"

"I'm sure of it, and of course you needn't tell me, you dearest dear—and we might begin with just a little lunch to-day. The breakfast was horrid, and I didn't get half enough even of what there was."

"But I must say now," Mr. Port went on—keenly regretting the unfortunate beginning that he had given to his declaration of independence, but judiciously ignoring Dorothy's shrewd perversion of it —"that your several suggestions literally are impossibilities. I admit that dancing for a short period, at about an hour after each meal, is an admirable exercise that produces a most salutary effect upon the digestive apparatus; but persistent dancing until an unduly late period of the night is a practice as unhygienic as, in the mixed company of a watering-place, it is socially objectionable.

"Tennis is an absurdity worthy of the vacuous minds of those who engage in it. To suggest that I shall sit in a cramped position in a draughty gallery for several hours at a stretch in order to watch empty-headed young men playing a perverted form of battledoor and shuttlecock across a net, is to imply that they and I are upon the same intellectual level; and this, I trust, is not the case.

"As you certainly should remember, Dorothy, all persons of a bilious habit suffer severely from seasickness; a fact that, of course, disposes effectually of your yachting plans. For you are not desirous, I am sure, of purchasing your own selfish enjoyment —if you possibly can have enjoyment on board a yacht—at the cost of my intense personal misery.

"But in regard to the lunches, my dear"—Mr. Port's tone softened perceptibly—"there certainly is something to be said. The food here at the hotel, I admit, is atrocious, and at the Casino it is possible occasionally to procure something eatable. Yes, I shall have much pleasure in giving a lunch this very morning to my angel" (Mr. Port, warming in advance under the genial influence of the croquette and salad that he intended to order, became playful), "for what you said in regard to the breakfast, Dorothy, was quite true—it was abominable. If you will excuse me, I will just step down to the Casino now and give my order; then things will be all ready for us when we get back from the bath."

And such was Miss Lee's generalship that she rested content with her success in one direction, and deferred until a more convenient season her further demands. She was a reasonable young woman, and was quite satisfied with accomplishing one thing at a time.

V.

Two or three days later Dorothy advanced her second parallel. In the interval they had bathed every morning and had driven to the Point every afternoon, and they had held converse upon the veranda of the hotel every evening until ten o'clock with certain eminently respectable people from Philadelphia, by whom Dorothy was bored, as she did not hesitate to confess, almost to desperation. Further, Mr. Port had given a lunch-party to which these same Philadelphians were invited; and his niece had informed him, when the festivity was at an end, that if he did anything like that again she certainly would either run away or drown herself. Any trials in this world or any dangers in the next, she declared, were preferable to sitting opposite to such a person as Mrs. Logan Rittenhouse, who talked nothing but uninteresting scandal and crochet, and next to Mr. Pennington Brown, who talked only about peoples' great-grandfathers and great-aunts.

It was with a lively alarm that Mr. Port noted these signs of discontent, together with returning symptoms of the grumpiness which had disturbed his comfort and digestion at Saratoga; and it was most selfishly in his own self-interest that he tried to think of something that would afford his niece amusement. Miss Lee, when she perceived that her intelligently laid plans were working successfully, was graciously pleased to assist him.

"It is a great pity, Uncle Hutchinson," she vouchsafed to remark on the fourth day of suppressed domestic sunshine, "that you don't like tennis. Don't you think, for your angel's sake, that you could go for just a little while this afternoon? There's going to be a capital match this afternoon, and your angel does so want to see it. You haven't been very—very agreeable the past two or three days, you dear, and I fear that your liver must be a little out of order. Really, you haven't given your angel a single chance to be affectionate—and unless she can be affectionate and sweet and clinging, and things like that, you know, your poor angel is not happy at all. Suppose we try the tennis for just half an hour or so? It won't be much of a sacrifice for you, and it will make your angel so happy that she will make herself dearer to you than ever, you precious thing."

This form of address was disconcerting to Mr. Port, for during the period to which Miss Lee referred he certainly had been trying—not very cleverly, perhaps, for such efforts were not at all in his line, but still to the best of his ability—to make himself as agreeable as possible; and the effort on the part of his niece to be angelic, of which she spoke so confidently, he could not but think had fallen rather more than a little short of absolute success. The one ray of comfort that he extracted from Dorothy's utterance was her reference to herself as his angel; he had come to understand that the use of this term was a sign of fair weather, and he valued it accordingly. But even for the sake of fair weather Mr. Port was not yet prepared to expose his elderly joints to the draughty discomforts of the galleries overhanging the tennis-court; and he said so, pretty decidedly. Almost anything else he was willing to do, he added, but that particular thing he would not do at all.

"As you please, Uncle Hutchinson," Dorothy answered, in a tone of gloomy resignation. "I am used to hearing that. It is just what poor dear mamma used to say. She always was willing, you know, to do everything but the thing that I wanted her to do. I remember, just to mention a single instance, how mamma broke up a delightful water party on Windermere that Sir Gordon Graham had arranged expressly for us. The weather was rather misty, as it is apt to be up there, you know, but nothing worth minding when you are well wrapped up. But mamma said that if she went out in such a drizzle she knew her cough would be ever so much worse—and of course she couldn't really know that it would be worse, for nobody truly knows what the weather is going to do to them—and so she wouldn't go. And Sir Gordon was very much hurt about it, and never came near us again. And unless I'm very much mistaken, Uncle Hutchinson, mamma's selfishness that day lost me the chance of being Lady Graham. So I'm used to being treated in this way, and you needn't at all mind refusing me everything that I ask." And, being delivered of this discourse, Miss Lee lapsed into a condition of funereal gloom.

At the end of another twenty-four hours Mr. Port knuckled under. "I have been thinking, Dorothy," he said, "about what you were saying about tennis. It's a beastly game, but since you insist upon seeing it I'll take you for a little while this afternoon." This was not the most gracious form of words in which an invitation could be couched; but Dorothy, who was not a stickler for forms provided she was successful in results, accepted it with alacrity. Later in the day, as they returned from the Casino, she declared:

"Your angel has had a lovely afternoon, Uncle Hutchinson, and she is sure that you have had a lovely afternoon too. And now that you've found what fun there is in looking at tennis, we'll go every day, won't we, dear? Sometimes, you know, you are just a little, just a very little prejudiced about things; but you are so good and sweet-tempered that your prejudices never last long, and so your angel cannot help loving you a great deal."

Mr. Port, who was not at all sweet-tempered at that moment, was prepared to reply to the first half of this speech in terms of some emphasis; for he was limping a little, and a shocking twinge took him in his left shoulder when he attempted to raise his arm. But Dorothy's sudden shifting to polite personalities was of a nature to choke off his projected indignant utterance. Yet not feeling by any means

prepared to meet in kind her pleasing manifestation
of affection, Mr. Port was a little put to it to find
any suitable form of response.   After a moment's
reflection he abandoned the attempt to reply cohe-
rently, and contented himself with grunting.

VI.

Encouraged by the success that was attending
her unselfish efforts to harmonize her own and her
uncle's conceptions of the temporal fitness of things,
Miss Lee began to find life at the Pier quite sup-
portable.   "There's not much to do here," she declared, with her customary candor, "and the hotels
—all ugly and all in a row—make it look like an
overgrown charitable institution ; and most of the
people, I must say, are such a dismal lot that they
might very well be the patients out for an airing.
But, on the whole, I've been in several worse places,
Uncle Hutchinson ; and if only you'd take me to a
hop now and then, instead of sitting every evening
on the pokey hotel veranda talking Philadelphia
twaddle with that stuffy old Mr. Pennington Brown,
I might have rather a good time here."

"You will oblige me, Dorothy," replied Mr. Port,
"by refraining from using such a word as 'stuffy'
in connection with a gentleman who belongs to one
of the oldest and best families in Philadelphia, and
who, moreover, is one of my most esteemed friends."

"*And before Mr. Port could rally his forces they had entered the carriage and had driven away.*"

"But he *is* stuffy, Uncle Hutchinson. He never talks about anything but who peoples' grandfathers and grandmothers were ; and *Watson's Annals* seems to be the only book that he ever has heard of. Indeed, I do truly think that he is the very stuffiest and stupidest old gentleman that I ever have known."

Mr. Port made no reply to this sally, for his feelings were such that he deemed it best not to give expression to them in words ; but he was not unnaturally surprised, after such a declaration of sentiments on the part of his niece, when she begged to be excused on the ensuing afternoon from her regular drive to the Point, on the ground that she had promised to make an expedition to the Rocks in Mr. Brown's company. Had an opportunity been given him Mr. Port would have asked for an explanation of this phenomenon ; but the carriage was in waiting that was to convey his ward and her extraordinary companion to the end of the road at Indian Rock—a slight rheumatic tendency, that he declared was hereditary, rendering it advisable for Mr. Brown to reduce the use of his legs to a minimum—and before Mr. Port could rally his forces they had entered it and had driven away.

In the evening Mr. Port found another surprise awaiting him. Miss Lee presently retired from the veranda for the avowed purpose of searching for a missing fan, thus leaving the two gentlemen together.

"What a charming girl your niece is, Port !" said Mr. Brown, as the fluttering train of Dorothy's dress disappeared through the door-way.

Mr. Port evidently considered that this possibly debatable statement was sufficiently answered by a grunt, for that was all the answer he gave it.

Not permitting his enthusiasm to be checked by this chillingly dubious response, Mr. Brown continued :

"She certainly is one of the most charming girls I have met in a long time, Port. She is not a bit like the average of young girls nowadays. I rarely have known a young person of either sex to be so genuinely interested in genealogy, especially in Philadelphia genealogy ; and I must say that her liking for antiquarian matters generally is very remarkable. I envy you, I really envy you, old boy, the blessing of that sweet young creature's constant companionship."

"Umph—do you?" was Mr. Port's concise and rather discouraging reply.

"Indeed I do"—Mr. Brown was too warm to notice the cynical tone of his friend's rejoinder—"and I have been thinking, Port, that we are a pair of selfish old wretches to monopolize every evening in the way that we have been doing this bright young flower. It is a shame for us to keep her in our stupid company—though she tells me that she finds our talk about old people and old times exceedingly interesting—instead of letting her have a little of the young society and a little of the excitement and pleasure of watering-place life. Now, how would it do for us to take her down to the Casino to-night ? There is to be a hop to-night, she says ; at least, that

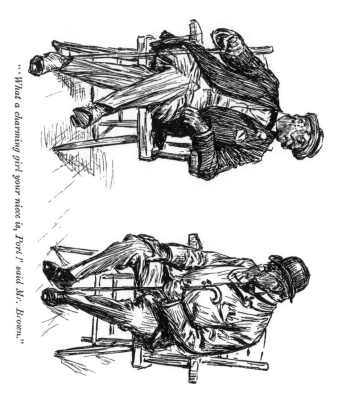

"'What a charming girl your niece is, Port!' said Mr. Brown."

is to say "—Mr. Brown became somewhat confused —" I heard somewhere that there is to be a hop to-night, and while that sort of thing is pretty stupid for you and me, it isn't a bit stupid for a young and pretty girl like her. So suppose we take her, old man ?"

As this amazing proposition was advanced by his elderly friend, Mr. Port's anger and astonishment were aroused together ; and his rude rejoinder to it was : " Have you gone crazy, Brown, or has Dorothy been making a fool of you ? Has she asked you to ask me to take her to the Casino hop ? She knows there is no use in talking to me about it any longer."

" No, certainly not—at least—that is to say—well, no, not exactly," replied Mr. Brown, beginning his sentence with an asperity and positiveness that some-how did not hold out to its end. " She did say to me, I confess, how fond she was of dancing, and how she had refrained from saying much about it to you " —Mr. Port here interpolated a sceptical snort—" be-cause she knew that taking her to the Casino would only bore you. And I do think, Port, that keeping her here with us all the time is grossly selfish ; and if you don't want to take her to the hop I hope you'll let her go with me. But what we'd better do, old man, is to take her together—then we can talk to each other just as well, at least nearly as well, as we can here, and we can have the comfort of knowing that she is enjoying herself too. Come, Hutch ; we're getting old and rusty, you and I, but let us try at least to keep from degenerating into a pair of selfish old brutes with no care for anybody's comfort but our own."

Mr. Hutchinson Port might have replied with a fair amount of truth that so far as he himself was concerned the degeneration that his friend referred to as desirable to avoid already had taken place. But all of us like most to be credited with the virtues of which we have least, and he therefore accepted as his due Mr. Brown's tribute of implied praise. And the upshot of the matter was that Dorothy, when she returned to the veranda again, was unaffectedly surprised (and considering how carefully she had planned her small campaign she did it very creditably) by discovering that her uncle's edict against the Casino hops had been withdrawn.

VII.

Even Dorothy was disposed to believe that unless some peculiarly favorable combination of circumstances presented itself as a basis for her intelligent manipulation her strong desire for a yacht voyage must remain ungratified; for, now that his liver was decidedly the larger part of him, Mr. Port had a fairly catlike dread of the sea. To be sure, Dorothy's character was a resolute one, and her staying powers were quite remarkable; but in the matter of venturing his bilious body upon the ocean she discovered that her uncle—although now reduced to a

fairly satisfactory state of submission in other re-
spects—had a large and powerful will of his own.

Fortune, however, favors the resolute even more
decidedly than she favors the brave. This fact Dorothy comprehended thoroughly, and uniformly acted
upon. Each time that even a remote possibility of
a yacht cruise presented itself she instantly brought
her batteries to bear ; and, with a nice understanding
of her uncle's intellectual peculiarities, she each time
treated the matter as though it never before had
been discussed.

Therefore it was that when Miss Lee's eyes were
gladdened one day—just as she and her uncle were
about to begin their lunch on the shady veranda of
the Casino — by the sight of a trim schooner yacht
sliding down the wind from the direction of New-
port, the subject of the cruise was revived with a sud-
denness and point that Mr. Port found highly disconcerting. The yacht rounded to off the Casino, and
the sound of a plunge and a clanking chain floated
across the water as her anchor went overboard.

"Oh, isn't she a beauty !" exclaimed Dorothy,
with enthusiasm. "Now, Uncle Hutchinson, her
owner is coming ashore—they have just brought the
gig round to the gangway—and if you don't know
him you must get somebody to introduce you to
him; and then you must introduce him to me; and
then he will ask us to go on a cruise; and of course
we will go, and have just the loveliest time in the
world. I haven't been on board a yacht for nearly
five years (just look at the gig: don't the men pull

3

splendidly ?)—not since that nice little Lord Alder-
hone took poor dear mamma and me up to Norway.
We did have such a good time! Poor dear mamma,
of course, was desperately sick—she always was horribly sea-sick, you know; but I'm never sea-sick the
least bit, and it was perfectly delightful. Look, Uncle Hutchinson, they've made the dock, and now he's
coming right up here. What a handsome man he
is, and how well he looks in his club uniform! It
seems to me I've seen him somewhere. Do you
know him, Uncle Hutchinson ?"

A serious difficulty under which Mr. Port labored
in his dealings with his niece was his inability—due
to his Philadelphia habit of mind—to keep up with
the exceptionally rapid flow of her ideas. On the
present occasion, while he still was engaged in consideration of the irrational proposition that he should
court the desperate misery that attends a bilious man
at sea by as good as asking to be taken on a yacht
voyage, he suddenly found his ideas twisted off into
another direction by the reference to his sister's suf-
ferings on a similar occasion in the past; and before he could frame in words the reproof that he was
disposed to administer to Dorothy for what he probably would have styled her heartlessness, he found
his thoughts shunted to yet another track by a direct question. It is within the bounds of possibility
that Miss Lee had arrived at a just estimate of her
relative's intellectual peculiarities, and that she even
sometimes framed her discourses with a view to taking advantage of them.

" The yacht rounded to off the casino."

The direct question being the simplest section of Dorothy's complex utterance, Mr. Port abandoned his intended remonstrance and reproof and proceeded to answer it. "Yes," he said, "I know him. It's Van Rensselaer Livingstone. His cousin, Van Ruyter Livingstone, married your cousin Grace—Grace Winthrop, you know. He's a great scamp—this one, I mean; gambles, and that sort of thing, I'm told, and drinks, and—and various things. I shall have to speak to him if he sees me, I suppose; but of course I shall not introduce him to you."

"Mr. Van Rensselaer Livingstone! Why so it is! How perfectly delightful! I know him very well, Uncle Hutchinson. He was in Nice the last winter we were there; and he broke the bank at Monaco; and he played that perfectly absurd trick on little Prince Sporetti: cut off his little black mustache when Prince Sporetti was—was not exactly sober, you know, and gummed on a great red mustache instead of it; and then, before the prince was quite himself again, took him to Lady Ormsby's ball. All Nice was in a perfect roar over it. And they had a duel afterwards, and Mr. Livingstone—he is a wonderful shot—instead of hurting the little prince, just shot away the tip of his left ear as nicely as possible. Oh, he is a delightful man—and here he comes." And Dorothy, half rising from her chair, and paying no more attention to Mr. Port's kicks under the table than she did to his smothered verbal remonstrances, extended her well-shaped white hand in the most cordial manner, and in the most cordial tone exclaimed:

"Won't you speak to me in English, Mr. Livingstone? We talked French, I think it was, the last
time we met. And how is your friend Prince Sporetti? Has his ear grown out again? You know
my uncle, I think? Mr. Hutchinson Port."

Livingstone took the proffered hand with even
more cordiality than it was given, and then extended his own to Mr. Port—who seemed much less in-
clined to shake it than to bite it.

"I think that we are justified in regarding ourselves as relations now, Miss Lee, since our cousins
have married each other, you know. Quite a romance, wasn't it? And how very jolly it is to meet
you here — when I thought that you certainly were
in Switzerland or Norway, or even over in that new
place that people are going to in Roumania! I flat-
ter myself that I always have rather a knack of falling on my feet, but, by Jove, I'm doing it more than
usual this morning!"

Miss Lee seemed to be entirely unaware of the
fact that her uncle was looking like an animated
thunder-cloud. "It is just like a bit out of a delightful novel," was her encouraging response. "A
long, low, black schooner suddenly coming in from
the seaward and anchoring close off shore, and the
hero landing in a little boat just in time to slay the
villain and rescue the beautiful bride. Of course
I'm the beautiful bride, but my uncle is not a villain,
but the very best of guardians—by-the-way, I don't
think that you know that poor dear mamma is dead,
Mr. Livingstone? Yes, she died only a week or two

after you left us. So you see you must be very nice to the villain — and you can begin your kind treatment of him by having lunch with him and with me too. Uncle Hutchinson was *so* pleased when he saw you come ashore. He said that we certainly must capture you, and he sent a man to bring some hot soup for you at once — here it is now." And so it was, for Dorothy herself very thoughtfully had given the order that she now modestly attributed to her uncle.

And so in less than ten minutes from the moment when Mr. Port had informed Dorothy that Van Rensselaer Livingstone was a very objectional person whom he desired to avoid, and whose introduction to her was not even to be thought of, they all three were lunching together in what to the casual observer seemed to be the most amicable manner possible.

VIII.

"I've run over to look up Mrs. Rattleton," said Livingstone, as he discussed with evident relish the *filet* that Mr. Port charitably hoped would choke him. "Very likely you haven't met her, for she's only just got here. But you'll like her, I know, for she's ever so jolly. She's promised to play propriety for me in a party that we want to make up aboard the yacht. The squadron won't get down from New York for a week yet, and I've come up ahead of it so that we can have a cruise to the Shoals and back before the races. Of course, Miss Lee, you won't fly in the face of Fate, after this providential meeting, by refusing to join our party; at least if you do you will make me wretched to the end of my days. And we will try to make you comfortable on board, sir," he added, politely, turning to Mr. Port. "I have a tolerably fair cook, and ice isn't the only thing in the ice-chest, I assure you."

"How very kind you are, Mr. Livingstone," Dorothy hastened to say, in order to head off her uncle's inevitable refusal. "Of course we will go, with the greatest possible pleasure. It is very odd how things fall out sometimes. Now only this morning I was begging Uncle Hutchinson to take me off yachting, and he was saying how much he enjoyed being at sea, and how he really thought that if it wasn't for his age — wasn't it absurd of him to talk about his age? He is not old at all, the dear!—he would have a yacht of his own. And almost before the words are fairly out of our mouths here you drop from the clouds, or are cast up by the sea, it's all the same thing, and give us both just what we have been longing for. At least, Uncle Hutchinson pretended to be longing for it only in case he could be young enough to enjoy it; but if he doesn't think he's young now, I'd like to know what he'll call himself when he's fifty!" And then, facing around sharply upon her uncle, Dorothy concluded: "The idea of pretending that *you* are too old to go yachting! Really, Uncle Hutchinson, I am ashamed of you!"

As has been intimated, if there was any one subject upon which Mr. Port was especially sensitive, it
was the subject of his age. As the parish register
of St. Peter's all too plainly proved, he never would
see sixty again; but this awkward record was in an
out-of-the-way place, and the agreeable fiction that
he advanced in various indirect ways to the effect
that he was a trifle turned of forty - seven was not
likely to be officially contradicted. And it is not
impossible, so tenacious was he upon this point, that
had the official proof been produced, he would have
denied its authenticity. For it was Mr. Port's firm
determination still to figure before the world as a
youngish, middle-aged man.

To say that Miss Lee deliberately set herself to
playing upon this weakness of her guardian's, possibly, remotely possibly, would be doing her injustice.
But the fact is obvious that she succeeded by her
cleverly turned discourse in landing her esteemed
relative fairly between the horns of an exceedingly
awkward dilemma: either Mr. Port must accept the
invitation and be horribly ill, or he must reject it,
and so throw over his pretensions to elderly youth.

For a moment the unhappy gentleman hung in the
wind, and Dorothy regretted that she had not made
her statement of the case still stronger. Indeed, she
was about to supplement it by a remark to the effect
that people never thought of giving up yachting until they were turned of sixty, when, to her relief, her
uncle slowly filled away on the right tack. His acceptance was expressed in highly ungracious terms;

but, as has been said, Dorothy never troubled herself about forms, provided she compassed results. The moment that he had uttered the fatal words, Mr. Port fell to cursing himself in his own mind for being such a fool; but the same reason that had impelled him to give his consent withheld him from retracting it. He knew that he was going to be desperately miserable; but, at least, nobody could say that he was old.

"I'm ever so much obliged to you, Miss Lee, and to you too, Mr. Port," said Livingstone. "And now, if you'll excuse me, I'll go and hunt up Mrs. Rattleton, and tell her what a splendid raise I've made, and help her organize the rest of the party. We shall have only two more. It's a bore to have more than six people on board a yacht. I don't know why it is, I'm sure, but if you have more than six they always get to fighting. Queer, isn't it?"

"I beg your pardon," said Mr. Port. "Mrs. Rattleton? May I ask if this is the Mrs. Rattleton from New York who was here last season, the one whose bathing costume was so — so very eccentric, and about whom there was so much very disagreeable talk?"

"Mrs. Rattleton *is* from New York, and she *was* here last season," Livingstone answered. "But I can't say that I remember anything eccentric in her bathing costume, except that it was exceedingly becoming; and I certainly never heard any disagreeable talk about her. There may have been such talk about her, but perhaps it was thought just as well not to have it in my presence. Mrs. Rattleton is my cousin, Mr. Port—she was a Van Twiller, you know. Do you happen to remember any of the things that were said about her, and who said them ?" Livingstone spoke with extreme courtesy ; but there was something in his tone that caused Mr. Port suddenly to think of the tip of Prince Sporetti's left ear, and that led him to reply hurriedly, and by no means lucidly :

" Certainly—no—yes—that is to say, I can't exactly remember anything in particular. I'm sure I was led to believe from what was said that she was a very charming woman. No, I don't remember at all."

"Ah, perhaps it is just as well," Livingstone replied, gravely. " But how lucky !" he added; " there she is now. Everybody is at the Casino about this time of day, I fancy. May I bring her over and present her to you, Miss Lee ?"

" Of course you may, Mr. Livingstone. I shall be delighted to meet her. And if she is to matronize me, the sooner that I begin to get accustomed to her severities the better."

And then Mr. Hutchinson Port suffered a fresh pang of misery when the presentation was accomplished and he was forced to say approximately pleasant things to a lady whose decidedly ballet-like attire in the surf—or, to be precise, on the beach above high-water-mark, where, for some occult reason, she usually saw fit to do the most of her bathing—joined to the exceeding celerity of her con-

duct generally, had marked her during the preceding
season as the conspicuous centre of one phase of life
at the Pier.   Nor was Mr. Port's lot made happier
as he listened to the brisk discussion that ensued in
regard to the organization of the yachting party,
and found that its two remaining members were to
be drawn, as was only natural, from the eminently
meteoric set to which Mrs. Rattleton belonged.

Had time been given Mr. Port for consideration
it is probable that he would have collected his mental forces sufficiently to have enabled him to lodge a
remonstrance; he might even—though this is doubtful, for Dorothy's voting power was vigorous—have
accomplished a veto.   But projects in which Mrs.
Rattleton was concerned never went slowly ; and in
the present case the necessity for getting back in
time for the races really compelled haste.   And so
it came to pass that not until the *Fleetwings* was off
the Brenton's Reef light-ship, with her nose pointed
well up into the north-east, was there framed in Mr.
Port's slow-moving mind a suitable line of argument upon which to base a peremptory refusal to
go upon the expedition—and by that time he was
so excruciatingly ill in his own cabin that coherent
utterance and converse with his kind were alike impossible.

So far as Mr. Port was concerned the ensuing six
days made up an epoch in his life that can only be
described as an agonized blank.   And when—as it
seemed to him many ages later—the *Fleetwings* once
more cast anchor off Narragansett Pier, and he step-

ped shakily from the schooner's gig to the Casino
dock, the usual plumpness and ruddiness of his face
had given place to a yellow leanness, and his weight
had been reduced by very nearly twenty pounds.
The cruise had been a flying one, or he never would
have finished it. After the first six hours he would
have landed on a desert island cheerfully—and it is
not impossible that a hint from Dorothy as to her
uncle's probable movements should a harbor be made
had induced Livingstone to give the land a wide
berth.

Dorothy came ashore blooming. "You don't know,
Uncle Hutchinson," she said, "what a perfectly lovely time I've had "—and this cheerful assertion was
the literal truth, for Mr. Port had entered his cabin
before the yacht had crossed the line between Bea-
ver Tail and Point Judith, and had not emerged
from it until the anchor went overboard. "And
you don't know," Miss Lee went on with effusion,
"how grateful your angel is to you for helping her
to have such a delightful cruise. I'm sorry that
you haven't been very well, Uncle Hutchinson; but
I know that you will be all the better for it. Poor
dear mamma, you know, was bilious too, and going
to sea always made her wretched; but she used to
be wonderfully well always when she got on shore
again. And you'll be wonderfully well too, you
dear; and that will be your reward for helping your
angel to have such a perfectly delightful time."

Mr. Port made no reply to this address, for his
condition of collapse was too complete to permit

him to give form in words to the thoughts of rage
and resentment which were burning in the depths
of his injured soul. Without a word to one single
member of the party, he climbed heavily into a carriage and was driven directly to his hotel—while
Dorothy, still under the chaperonage of Mrs. Rattleton, gayly joined the pleasant little lunch-party at
the Casino with which the yacht voyage came to an
end.

IX.

During the ensuing week, a considerable portion
of which Mr. Port passed in the privacy of his own
room, the relations between Miss Lee and her guardian were characterized by a chill formality that
was ominous of a coming storm. In point of fact,
Mr. Port was waiting only until he should fully regain his strength in order to try conclusions with
Dorothy once and for all—and he was most highly
resolved that in the impending battle royal he should
not suffer defeat. So far, he had gone down in each
encounter with his spirited antagonist because the
tactics employed against him were of an unfamiliar
sort. But he was beginning to get the hang of these
tactics now ; and he also had got what in fighting
parlance would have been styled his second wind.
As he thought of the wrongs which had been heaped
upon him, rage filled his breast ; and the strong determination slowly shaped itself within him that to

the finesse of the enemy he would oppose a solid front of brute force.

Astuteness was not the least marked of Miss Lee's many charming characteristics, and although her guardian gave no outward sign of his belligerent intentions, she felt an inward conviction that a decisive trial of strength between them was at hand. Five or six years earlier she had engaged in a trial of this nature with her mother, and had emerged from it victorious. In that case, feminine weakness had yielded to feminine strength. But now the gloomy thought assailed her that her uncle, while closely resembling her mother in the matter of his liver, had in the depths of his torpid nature a substratum of brutal masculine resolution against which, should it fairly be set in array, she might battle in vain. And the upshot of her meditations was the conviction that her only chance of success lay in avoiding a battle by a radical change of base.

An easy way, as she perceived, to effect such a change of base was to marry Van Rensselaer Livingstone. Indeed, his proposal, a couple of days after the yacht voyage ended, came so opportunely that she almost was surprised into accepting it out of hand. But Dorothy was too well balanced a young person to do anything hastily, even to get herself out of a tight place; and while she held Livingstone's proposal under advisement—as a line of retreat kept open for use in case of urgent necessity —she welcomed it less for the possibilities of a safer position that it offered than for those which it suggested to her fertile mind.

Marriage, she decided, was the only way by which she could score a final victory over her uncle, and at the same time spike his guns; but it did not necessarily follow that her marriage must be with Livingstone. Indeed, as her coolly intelligent mind perceived, marrying an unmanageable young man in order to be free of an unmanageable old one would be simply walking out of the frying-pan into the fire—and that was not at all the resolution of her difficulties that Dorothy sought. The plan that now began to shape itself in her mind was one by which both fire and frying-pan would be successfully avoided; and as the more that she examined into it the more desirable it appeared to her, she lost no time in carrying it into effect—whereby, in less than three days' time, she sent Mr. Van Rensselaer Livingstone away in such a rage that he put to sea in the very face of a threatening north-easter, and in a much shorter period she caused her uncle seriously to doubt the evidence of his own senses.

At the end of his week of retirement, Mr. Port found himself in the hale condition of a bilious giant refreshed with blue-pills. He looked a little thinner than when he had started upon his ill-starred cruise, and his usual ruddiness was not as yet fully restored; but he was in capital condition, and a good deal more than ready for Miss Lee to come on. He could not very well, in the nature of the case, start an offensive campaign; but at the very first sug-

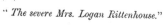

" The severe Mrs. Logan Rittenhouse."

gestion on Dorothy's part of the slightest desire to engage again in any of the various forms of frivolous amusement by which she had made his life a burden to him, he was all loaded and primed to go off with a bang that he believed would settle her.

And, such is the perversity of human nature, Mr. Port presently became not a little annoyed by Dorothy's failure to supply the spark that was to touch him off. In fact, her conduct was bewilderingly strange. She drew away from the lively circle of which Mrs. Rattleton was the animated centre and voluntarily associated herself with the elderly and very respectable Philadelphians whose acquaintance she previously had so emphatically declined. Still further to Mr. Port's astonishment, the lady and gentleman especially singled out by Miss Lee as most in accord with her newly-acquired tastes were the severe Mrs. Logan Rittenhouse and that lady's staid brother, Mr. Pennington Brown. At the feet of the former, quite literally, she sat as a disciple in crochet; and listened the while with every outward sign of interest to the dull record of South Fourth Street scandals of the past and West Walnut Street scandals of the present which this estimable matron poured into her ears by the hour at a time. And in a quiet corner of the veranda (Mr. Brown's eyesight having failed a little, so that he found reading rather difficult) she read aloud to the latter from *Watson's Annals;* and listened with a pleased satisfaction to his comments upon her selections from this, the Philadelphia Bible, and to the numerous anecdotes of a

genealogical and antiquarian cast which thus were
recalled to his mind.   Possibly the readings from
Watson were continued in the afternoons — when
Miss Lee and Mr. Brown regularly went down to
the Rocks.   So extraordinary was all this that Mr.
Port admitted frankly to himself that he could
make neither head nor tail of it; but he had an inborn conviction that such an unnatural state of
affairs was not likely to last.   There was good
Scriptural authority, he called to mind grimly, for
the assertion that the leopard did not change his
spots nor the Ethiopian his skin.

X.

In accordance with the substantial customs of his
fellow-citizens, Mr. Port always returned to Philadelphia sharp on the 1st of September—calmly ignoring the heat and the mosquitoes, which are the
dominant characteristics of Phildelphia during that
month, and resting secure in the knowledge that the
course which he pursued was that which his father
and his grandfather had pursued before him.   It
was on the eve of his departure from Narragansett
that his doubts and perplexities occasioned by Dorothy's surprising conduct were resolved.

Being seated in a snug corner of the veranda in
company with Mr. Pennington Brown, Mr. Port was
smoking a comforting cigar.   Mr. Brown, who also

was smoking, did not seem to find his cigar comforting. He smoked it in so fitful a fashion that it repeatedly went out; and his nervousness seemed to be increased each time that he lighted it. Further, his comment upon Mr. Port's discourse—which was a more than ordinarily thoughtful and accurate weighing of the relative merits of thin and thick soups—obviously were delivered quite at random. At first Mr. Port was disposed to resent this inattention to his soulful utterances; but as the subject was one in which, as he well knew, his friend was profoundly interested, he presently became uneasy.

"What's the matter, Brown?" he asked, in a tone of kindly concern. "Is your rheumatism bothering you? I've been afraid that your absurd sitting around on rocks with my niece would bring it on again. You're not as young as you once were, Pen, and you've got to take care of yourself."

"I am not aware, Port," Mr. Brown answered rather stiffly, "that I am as yet conspicuously superannuated. Indeed, I never felt younger in my life than I have felt during the past fortnight. I *have* a little touch of rheumatism to-night," he added, frankly, and at the same time gave unintentional emphasis to his admission by catching his breath and almost groaning as he slightly moved his legs, "but it has nothing to do with sitting on the rocks with Dor—with your charming niece. You forget that my rheumatism is hereditary, Port. Why, I had an attack of it when I was only five-and-twenty."

"All the same, you wouldn't have it now if you

4

had spent your afternoons sensibly with me here on a dry veranda, or properly wrapped up in a dry carriage, instead of on damp rocks, with that baggage. What on earth has got into you I can't imagine. If you were twenty years younger, Brown, I should think, yes, positively, I should think that you were in love with her."

"Port," said Mr. Brown, with a tone of resentment in his voice, "I shall be very much obliged if you will not use such language when you are speaking of Miss Lee. She is the best and kindest and noblest woman I ever have met. You have most cruelly misunderstood her. Had you given her half a chance she would have been to you only a source of constant joy."

Mr. Port replied to this emphatic assertion by a low, but most pointedly incredulous, whistle.

"You have not the slightest conception, as such a comment shows," Mr. Brown continued, with increasing asperity, "of the depths of sweetness and tenderness which are in her nature ; of her perfect unselfishness ; of the gentleness and trustfulness of her heart. She is all that a woman can be, and more. She is—she is an angel !" Mr. Brown's elderly voice trembled as he made this avowal.

As for Mr. Port, his astonishment was almost too deep for words. But he managed to say : "Yes, I suppose she is—at least she has said so often enough herself."

For some seconds there was silence ; and then, with a deprecating manner and in a voice from

which all trace of resentment had disappeared, Mr.
Brown resumed: "Hutch, old man, you and I have
been friends these many years together, and you
won't fail me in your friendship now, will you?
You are right, I *am* in love with this sweet young
creature, and she—think of it, Hutch!—she has admitted that she is in love with me; not romanti-
cally in love, for that would be, not absurd, of
course, but a little unreasonable—for while I'm not
at all old, yet I know, of course, that I am not exactly what can be called young—but in love sensibly and rationally. She wants to take care of me,
she says, the dear child!" (Mr. Port grunted.)
"And she has such clever notions in regard to my
health. When we are married—how strange and
how delightful it sounds, Hutch!—she says that we
will go immediately to Carlsbad, where the waters
will do my rheumatism a world of good; and from
there, when I am better, we will go on to Vienna,
where the dry climate and the white wines, she
thinks, still further will benefit me; and from Vienna, in order to set me on my feet completely, we
are to go on to the North and spend a winter in
Russia—for there is nothing that cures rheumatism
so quickly and so thoroughly, she says (though I
never should have imagined it) as steady and long-
continued cold. Just think of her planning it all
out for me so well!

"Yes, Hutch, I love her with all my heart; and
what has made me so nervous to-night is the great
happiness that has come to me—it only came posi-

tively this afternoon—and the dread that perhaps,
as her guardian, you know, you might not approve
of what we have decided to do. But you do approve, don't you, Hutch? Of course, in a few
months she will be her own mistress, and your consent to our marriage, as she very truly says, then
will be unnecessary. But even a month seems a
desperately long while to wait; and that is the very
shortest time, she thinks, in which she could get
ready—though the dear child has consented to wait
for most of the little things which she wants until
we get on the other side." Mr. Port smiled cyni-
cally at the announcement of this concession. It
struck him that when Dorothy was turned loose
among the Paris shops, backed by the capacious
purse of a doting elderly husband, she would mow
a rather startlingly broad swath. "So you won't
oppose our marriage, will you, old man? You will
consent to my having this dear young creature for
my wife?"

Various emotions found place in Mr. Port's breast
as he listened to this extraordinary declaration and
appeal. At first he felt a lively anger at Dorothy
for having, as he coarsely phrased it in his own
mind, so successfully gammoned Mr. Pennington
Brown; to this succeeded an involuntary admiration
of the clever way in which she had managed it; and
then a feeling of profound satisfaction possessed him
as there came into his slow-moving mind a realizing
sense of his own deliverance. But Mr. Port was not
so utterly selfish but that, in the midst of the sunrise

of happiness which dawned upon him with the opening of a way by which he decently could get rid of Dorothy, he was assailed by certain qualms of conscience as to the unfairness of thus casting upon his old friend the burden that he had found so hard to bear. For the heaviness of Mr. Port's mental processes prevented him from perceiving, as a shrewder person would have perceived, that Dorothy was not the sort of young woman to engage in an enterprise of this nature without first fully counting the cost. Had he been keener of penetration he would have known that she could be trusted, when safely landed in the high estate of matrimony, to play on skilfully the game that she had so skilfully begun; that in her own interest she would manage matters in such a way as never to arouse in the mind of her elderly husband the awkward suspicion that the scheme of life arranged by his angel apparently with a view solely to his own comfort really was arranged only for the comfort of her angelic self.

It was while Mr. Port wavered among his qualms of conscience, hesitating between his great longing to chuck Dorothy overboard, and so have done with her, and his sense of duty to Mr. Pennington Brown, that the subject of his perplexities herself appeared upon the scene; and her arrival at so critical a juncture seemed to suggest as a remote possibility that she had been all the while snuffing this particular battle from not very far off.

"Dear Uncle Hutchinson," said Miss Lee, with affectionate fervor, "do you think that your angel

is most cruel and horrid because she is willing to go
off in this way after her own selfish happiness and
leave you all alone? But she won't do it, dear, if
you would rather have her stay. Her only wish, you
know, has been to make you comfortable and happy;
and you have been so good and so kind to her that
she is ready to sacrifice even her love for your sake.
Yes, if you would rather keep her to yourself she
will stay. Only if she does stay," and there was a
warning tone of deep meaning in Miss Lee's well-
modulated voice, "her heart, of course, will be
broken, and she will have to ask you to travel with
her for two or three years into out-of-the-way parts
of the world" (Mr. Port shuddered) "until her poor
broken heart gets well. Not that it ever will get
quite well again, you know; but she will be brave,
and try to pretend for your sake that it has. So it
shall be just as you say, dear; only for Pennington's sake, who loves me so much, Uncle Hutchinson, I hope that perhaps you may be willing to let
me go."

And having concluded this moving address, Miss
Lee extended one of her well-shaped hands to Mr.
Pennington Brown—who grasped it warmly, for he
was deeply moved by so edifying an exhibition of
affectionate and dutiful unselfishness—and with the
other applied her handkerchief delicately to her eyes.

Mr. Port was not in the least moved by Dorothy's
professions of self-sacrifice; but he was most seriously alarmed by her threat—that opened before
him a dismal vista of bilious misery—to cart him

for several years about the world on the pretext of
a broken heart that required travel for its mending.
He believed, to be sure, that in a stand-up fight
he could conquer Dorothy; but he had his doubts as
to how long she would stay conquered—and between

constant fighting and constant travel there is not
much choice; for Mr. Port knew from experience
how acute is that form of biliousness which results
from rage. After all, self-preservation is the first
law of nature; and under the stress thus put upon

him, therefore, it is not surprising that Mr. Port's qualms of conscience incident to his failure to do his duty to his neighbor vanished to the winds.

Mr. Pennington Brown still held Dorothy's hand in his own. "Will you make this great sacrifice, Hutch, for your old friend?" he asked.

Mr. Port hesitated a little, for he felt a good deal like a criminal who is shifting his crime upon an innocent man; and then he answered, rather weakly both in tones and terms: "Why, of course."

"Dear Uncle Hutchinson, how good you are!" exclaimed Miss Lee. "And you really think that you can spare your angel, then?"

And both promptly and firmly Mr. Port answered: "Yes, I really think that I can."

A BORDER RUFFIAN.

I.—WEST.

I.

THROUGHOUT the whole of the habitable globe there nowhere is to be found more delightful or more invigorating air than that which every traveller through New Mexico, from Albuquerque, past Las Vegas, to the Raton Mountains, is free to breathe.

Miss Grace Winthrop, of Boston, and also Miss Winthrop, her paternal aunt, and also Mr. Hutchinson Port, of Philadelphia, her maternal uncle—all of whom were but forty hours removed from the Alkali Desert west of the Continental Divide—felt in the very depths of their several beings how entirely good this air was ; and, as their several natures moved them, they betrayed their lively appreciation of its excellence.

Miss Grace Winthrop, having contrived for herself, with the intelligent assistance of the porter, a most comfortable nest of pillows, suffered her novel to remain forgotten upon her knees ; and, as she leaned her pretty blond head against the wood-

work separating her section from that adjoining it,
looked out upon the brown mountains, and accorded
to those largely-grand objects of nature the rare
privilege of being reflected upon the retina of her
very blue eyes. Yet the mountains could not flat-
ter themselves with the conviction that contemplation of them wholly filled her mind, for occasionally
she smiled a most delightful smile.

Miss Winthrop, retired from the gaze of the world
in the cell that the Pullman-car people euphemistical-
ly style a state-room, ignored all such casual excres-
cences upon the face of nature as mountains, and
seriously read her morning chapter of Emerson.

Mr. Hutchinson Port, lulled by the easy, jog-trot
motion of the car, and soothed by the air from Paradise that, for his virtues, he was being permitted to
breathe, lapsed into calm and grateful slumber : and
dreamed (nor could a worthy Philadelphian desire a
better dream) of a certain meeting of the Saturday
Night Club, in December, 1875, whereat the terrapin
was remarkable, even for Philadelphia.

Miss Winthrop, absorbed in her Emersonian devo-
tions, and Mr. Hutchinson Port, absorbed in slumber, did not perceive that the slow motion of the
train gradually became slower, and finally entirely
ceased ; and even Grace, lost in her pleasant day-
dream, scarcely observed that the unsightly buildings
of a little way-station had thrust themselves into the
foreground of her landscape—for this foreground she
ignored, keeping her blue eyes serenely fixed upon
the great brown mountains beyond. Nor was she

more than dimly conscious of the appearance upon the station platform of a tall, broad-shouldered young man clad in corduroy, wearing a wide-brimmed felt-hat, and girded about with a belt, stuck full of cartridges, from which depended a very big revolver. In a vague way she was conscious of this young man's existence, and of an undefined feeling that, as the type of a dangerous and interesting class, his appearance was opportune in a part of the country which she had been led to believe was inhabited almost exclusively by cut-throats and outlaws.

In a minute or two the train went on again, and as it started Grace was aroused and shocked by the appearance at the forward end of the car of the ruffianly character whom she had but half seen from the car window. For a moment she believed that the train-robbery, that she had been confidently expecting ever since her departure from San Francisco, was about to take place. Her heart beat hard, and her breath came quickly. But before these symptoms had time to become alarming the desperado had passed harmlessly to the rear end of the car, and after him had come the porter carrying his valise and a Winchester rifle.

"Goin' to Otero? Yes, sah! All right, sah! Put yo' heah; nice seat on shady side, sah! Thank yo', sah! Have a pillow, sah?" And, hearing this address on the part of the porter, Grace knew that the desperado, for the moment at least, was posing in the character of a law-abiding citizen, and was availing himself of his rights as such to ride in a Pullman-car. Being thus relieved of cause for immediate alarm, her breast presently began to swell with a fine indignation at the impudence of this abandoned person in thus thrusting himself into a place reserved, if not absolutely for aristocratic, certainly, at least, for respectable society.

II.

The slight stir incident to the entrance of this offensive stranger aroused Mr. Hutchinson Port from his agreeable slumber. He yawned slightly, cast a disparaging glance upon the mountains, and then, drawing an especially good cigar from his case, betook himself to the smoking-room. Grace did not realize his intentions until they had become accomplished deeds.

Mr. Hutchinson Port—although a member (on the retired list) of the First City Troop, and therefore, presumably, inflamed with the martial spirit characteristic of that ancient and honorable organization— was not, perhaps, just the man that a person knowing in such matters would have selected to pit against a New Mexico desperado in a hand-to-hand conflict. But Grace felt her heart sink a little as she saw the round and rather pursy form of her natural protector walk away into the depths of a mirror at the forward end of the car, and so vanish. And in this same mirror she beheld, seated only two sections behind her, the scowling ruffian!

The situation, as Grace regarded it, was an alarming one; and it was the more trying to her nerves
because it did not, reasonably, admit of action. She
was aware that the very presence of a ruffian in a
Pullman car was in the nature of a promise, on his
part, that for the time being it was not his intention
either to murder or to rob—unless, indeed, he were
one of a robber band, and was awaiting the appearance of his confederates. For her either to call her
uncle, or break in upon the Emersonian seclusion of
her aunt, she felt would not be well received, under
the circumstances, by either of these her relatives.
As to the porter, that sable functionary had vanished; there was no electric bell, and the car, one of
a Pullman train, had no conductor.

For protection, therefore, should need for protection arise, Grace perceived that she must depend
upon the one other passenger. (They had lingered
so long amid the delights of a Santa Barbara spring
that they were journeying in that pleasant time of
year when spring travel eastward has ended, and
summer travel has not yet begun.) This one other
passenger was a little man of dapper build and dapper dress, whose curiously-shaped articles of luggage
betokened his connection with commercial affairs.
Grace was forced to own, as she now for the first
time regarded him attentively, that he did not seem
to be wrought of the stern stuff out of which, as a
rule, champions are made.

As she thus looked upon him, she was startled to
find that he was looking very fixedly upon her; and

she was further startled, as their eyes met, by the appearance upon his face of a friendly smile. She would have been vastly surprised had she been aware that this little person labored under the belief that he had already effected a favorable lodgement in her good graces; and she would have been both surprised and horrified could she have known that each of her own strictly confidential smiles during her day-dream had been accepted by the commercial traveller as intended for himself; and had been met, as they successively appeared, by his own smiles in answer. Yet this was the actual state of the case; and the little man's soul was uplifted by the thought that here was a fresh proof, and a very pleasant one, of how irresistible were his personal appearance and his personal charm of manner when arrayed in battery against any one of the gentler sex.

Viewed from the stand-point of his experience, this inquiring look and its attendant eye-encounter indicated that the moment for more pronounced action now had arrived. With the assured air of one who possibly may be repulsed, but who certainly cannot be defeated, he arose from his seat, crossed to Miss Grace Winthrop's section, and, with a pleasant remark to the effect that in travelling it always was nice to be sociable, edged himself into the seat beside her.

For a moment, the insolent audacity of this move was so overwhelming that Grace was quite incapable of coherent expression. The lovely pink of her cheeks became a deep crimson that spread to the very tips of her ears; her blue eyes flashed, and her hands clinched instinctively.

"Looked like a perfect little blue-eyed devil," the drummer subsequently declared, in narrating a highly-embellished version of his adventure, "but she didn't mean it, you know—at least, only for a minute or two. I soon combed her down nicely." What he actually said, was:

"Been travellin' far, miss?"

"What do you mean by this? Go away!" Grace managed to say; but she could not speak very clearly, for she was choking.

"Come, don't get mad, miss! I know you're not mad, really, anyway. When a woman's as handsome as you are, she can't be bad-natured. Come from California, I suppose? Nice country over there, ain't it?"

What with surprise and rage and fright, Grace was very nearly frantic. For the moment she was powerless—her uncle in the smoking-room, her aunt locked up with her Emersonian meditations, the porter in the lobby; the only available person upon whom she could call for aid a horrible drunken murderer and robber, steeped in all the darkest crimes of the frontier! She felt herself growing faint, but she struggled to her feet. The drummer laid his hand on her arm: "Don't go away, my dear! Just stay and have a little talk. You see—"

But the sentence was not finished. Grace felt her head buzzing, and then, from somewhere—a long way off, it seemed—she heard a voice saying: "I
5

beg your pardon; this thing seems to be annoying you. Permit me to remove it."

Her head cleared a little, for there was a promise of help not only in the words but in the tone. And then she saw the desperado calmly settle a big hand into the collar of the little man's coat, lift him out of the seat and well up into the air, and so carry him at arm's-length—kicking and struggling, and looking for all the world like a jumping-jack—out through the passage-way at the forward end of the car.

As they disappeared, she precipitately sought refuge in the state-room—where Miss Winthrop was aroused from her serious contemplation of All-pervading Thought by a sudden and most energetic demand upon her protection and her salts-bottle. And, before she could be made in the least degree to comprehend why Grace should require either the one or the other, Grace had still further complicated and mystified the matter by fainting dead away.

III.

In the course of two or three hours — aided by Miss Winthrop's salts and Mr. Hutchinson Port's travelling-flask of peculiar old Otard, which together contributed calmness and strength, and being refreshed by a little slumber—Grace was able to explain in an intelligible manner the adventure that had befallen her.

"And no matter what dreadful crimes that hor-

rible man may have committed," she said, in conclusion. "I shall be most grateful to him to my
dying day. And I want you, Uncle Hutchinson, no
matter how unpleasant it may be to you to do so, to
thank him from me for what he did. And, oh! it
was so funny to see that detestable little impudent
man kicking about that way in the air!" Which
remembrance, at the same moment, of both the ter-
rifying and the ludicrous side of her recent experience, not unnaturally sent Grace off into hysterics.

Mr. Hutchinson Port was quite ready to carry the
message of thanks to the desperado, and to add to
it some very hearty thanks of his own. But his
good intentions could not be realized; the desperado
no longer was on the train.

"Yes, sah; I knows the gen'l'm yo' means, sah,"
responded the porter, in answer to inquiries. Pow'fl
big gen'l'm yo' means, as got on this mo'nin' to Vegas. Thet's th' one, sah! He'd some kind er trib-
bilation with th' little gen'l'm'—th' drummer gen'l'm'
as got on las' night to Lamy—an' he brought him
out, holdin' him like he was a kitten, to the lobby,
an' jus' set him down an' boxed his ears till he hol-
lered! Yes, sah, thet's th' one. He got off to Otero.
An' th' little man he got off to Trinidad, an' said he
was agoin' up by the Denver to Pueblo. Yes, sah;
they's both got off, sah! Thank yo', sah! Get yo'
a pillow, sah?"

IV.

And so it came to pass that Miss Grace Winthrop returned to Boston cherishing towards desperadoes in general, and towards the desperadoes of New Mexico in particular, sentiments as generous as they were unusual.

Miss Winthrop the elder, whose soul was accustomed to a purer ether than that in which desperadoes ordinarily are found, presently forgot the vicarious excitements of her journey eastward in the calm joys of the Summer School of Philosophy.

And Mr. Hutchinson Port longed to be able to forget the whole State of California: when he realized, as he did with a most bitter keenness, that the superficial charms of that greatly overrated region had detained him upon the Western coast until the terrapin season was absolutely at an end!

II.—EAST.

The Incident of the Mysterious Stranger, and the Philadelphia Dinner-party.

I.

Mrs. Rittenhouse Smith had achieved righteousness. That is to say, being a Philadelphian, she was celebrated for giving successful dinners. The per-

son who achieves celebrity of this sort in Philadelphia is not unlike the seraph who attains to eminence
in the heavenly choir.

It was conceded that Mr. Rittenhouse Smith (he
was one of *the* Smiths, of course—not the others.
His mother was a Biddle) was an important factor
in his wife's success ; for, as became a well-brought-
up Philadelphian, he attended personally to the
marketing.   But had these Smith dinners been commendable only because the food was good, they
would not have been at all remarkable.   In Philadelphia, so far as the eating is concerned, a bad dinner seems to be an impossibility.

In truth, Mrs. Smith's dinners were famous because they never were marred by even the slightest
suggestion of a *contretemps;* because they glided
along smoothly, and at precisely the proper rate of
speed, from oysters to coffee ; and, because—and to
accomplish this in Philadelphia was to accomplish
something very little short of a miracle—they never
were stupid.

Therefore it was that Mrs. Rittenhouse Smith
stood among the elect, with a comfortable sense of
security in her election ; and she smelled with a
satisfied nose the smell of the social incense burned
before her shrine ; and she heard with well-pleased
ears the social hosannas which constantly were sung
in her praise.

II.

Occupying a position at once so ornate and so enviable, the feelings of Mrs. Rittenhouse Smith may be imagined upon finding herself confronted with the tragical probability that one of her most important dinner-parties would be a failure.

In preparing for this dinner-party she had thought deeply in the still watches of the night, and she had pondered upon it in the silence of noonday. For Mrs. Smith, above all others, knew that only by such soulful vigilance can a perfect dinner be secured. It was her desire that it should be especially bright intellectually, for it was to be given to Miss Winthrop, of Boston, and was to include Miss Winthrop's niece, Miss Grace Winthrop, also of Boston. These ladies, as she knew, belonged to clubs which, while modestly named after the days of the week, were devoted wholly to the diffusion of the most exalted mental culture. Moreover, they both were on terms of intimacy with Mr. Henry James. On the other hand, it was her desire that the dinner should be perfect materially, because among her guests was to be Miss Grace Winthrop's uncle, Mr. Hutchinson Port. It was sorely against Mrs. Smith's will that Mr. Hutchinson Port was included in her list, for he had the reputation of being the most objectionable diner-out in Philadelphia. His conversation at table invariably consisted solely of disparaging remarks, delivered in an undertone to his immediate neighbors, upon the character and quality of the food. However, in the present case, as Miss Grace Winthrop's uncle, he was inevitable.

And, such was Mrs. Smith's genius, she believed that she had mastered the situation. Her list—excepting, of course, Mr. Hutchinson Port, and he could not reasonably be objected to by his own relatives —was all that she could desire. The nine other guests, she was satisfied, were such as could be exhibited creditably even to ladies belonging to Boston clubs and personally acquainted with Mr. Henry James. As to the dinner itself, Mr. Rittenhouse Smith, who never spoke inconsiderately in matters of this grave nature, had agreed with her that—barring, of course, some Providentially interposed calamity such as scorching the ducks or getting too much salt in the terrapin—even Mr. Hutchinson Port would be unable to find a flaw in it.

And now, at the last moment, at twelve o'clock of the day on which the dinner was to take place, came a note from the man upon whom she had most strongly counted to make the affair a success—the brightest man on her list, and the one who was to take out Miss Grace Winthrop—saying that he was laid up with a frightful cold and face-ache! He tried to make a joke of it, poor fellow, by adding a sketch—he sketched quite nicely—of his swelled cheek swathed in a handkerchief. But Mrs. Rittenhouse Smith was in no humor for joking; she was furious !

When a woman misses fire in this way, it usually

is possible to fill her place with a convenient young sister, or even with an elderly aunt. But when a man is wanted, and, especially, as in the case in point, a clever man, the matter very readily may become desperate. Mrs. Rittenhouse Smith certainly was dismayed, yet was she not utterly cast down. She had faith in her own quick wits, which had rescued her in times past from other social calamities, though never from one darker than this, of having, at a single fatal blow, her best man cut off from one of her most important dinner-parties, and the dinner-party itself reduced to thirteen; an ominous and dismal number that surely would be discovered, and that would cast over her feast a superstitious gloom.

In this trying emergency Mrs. Smith acted with characteristic decision and wisdom. She perceived that to send invitations simultaneously to all the possible men of her acquaintance might involve her in still more awkward complications, while to send invitations successively might result in a fatal loss of time. Obviously, the only practicable course was a series of prompt, personal appeals from one to another, until assurance was received that the vacant place certainly would be filled. Therefore she despatched a note to Mr. Rittenhouse Smith, at his down-town office, acquainting him with the impending catastrophe and bidding him drop all other concerns until he had averted it by securing a satisfactory man.

III.

Now, under ordinary circumstances, Mr. Rittenhouse Smith would have obeyed his wife's orders cheerfully and promptly; but on this particular day there was a flurry in the stock-market (Mr. Smith was a stock-broker), and every minute that he was away from his office exposed him to serious business danger. At what he considered to be the safest moments, he made no less than five sallies after as many different men; and three of these had engagements for the evening, and two of them were out of town. What with the condition of the stock-market and the gloomy outlook for the dinner-party, Mr. Smith, albeit he was ordinarily a calm, sedate man, was almost distraught.

Three o'clock brought a prospect of relief, but after a day of such active dealing his books could not be settled hurriedly. In point of fact, when at last he was able to leave his Third Street office the State House clock was striking five; and the dinner, in accordance with Philadelphia custom, was to be at seven! He knew that his wife had discharged into his hands the matter of procuring the needed man; and he knew that this line of action on her part had been both right and wise; but he groaned in spirit, as he thought how dreadful a responsibility was his!

Mr. Smith was a methodical man, and in the calmness partly bred of his naturally orderly habits, and partly bred of his despair, he seated himself at his desk, in company with a comforting cigar, to think of any possible men whom he might beat up at their homes as he went westward. While he thus meditated—and while blackness settled down upon his soul, for of none could he think available for his purpose—he looked idly at the list of hotel arrivals in the morning paper that chanced to lie beside him; and suddenly he arose with a great shout of joy, for in this list he beheld the name, "Van R. Livingstone."

Here, indeed, was good-fortune at last! Van Rensselaer Livingstone was in college with him, in his own class, at Harvard. They had been capital friends while their college life lasted; and although Livingstone had spent the last ten or twelve years in Europe, they had not wholly lost track of each other. Clever, handsome, well-born, and well-bred, he was everything that the present occasion required. He seemed to have been sent from heaven direct. In twenty minutes Mr. Smith was asking for him at his hotel.

"Mr. Livingstone? Mr. Livingstone is out."

"Did he leave any word as to when he would come in?"

"Yes, sir. He said that a gentleman might call, and to say that he certainly would be back at six, and would not go out again to-night."

Mr. Smith looked at his watch—it was 5:30. Had there been any uncertainty as to Livingstone's return, he would have waited. But it was clear that he was coming back to dine at his hotel, and to spend the evening there. A note, therefore, could be trusted to do the business, and by writing, instead of waiting, Mr. Smith would save half an hour ; moreover, if he waited, he would not have time to make the mayonnaise.

Probably it is only in Philadelphia that it ever occurs nowadays to the master of a feast to dress the salad ; which, doubtless, is the reason why a better salad is served at certain dinner-tables in Philadelphia than at any other dinner-tables in the whole world.

The thought of the mayonnaise settled the matter. Mr. Smith hastily wrote an account of the trying situation, and concluded his note with a solemn demand upon "dear old Van" to fill the vacant place, "in the holy name of the class of '68, and for love of your old classmate, R. Smith."

IV.

Presently the person thus adjured returned to his hotel, and with a somewhat puzzled expression read the adjuration. "R. Smith," he murmured, reflectively. "I think I do remember a Dicky Smith, from Philadelphia, at Columbia. But he wasn't in my class, and my class wasn't '68, but '76, and I don't remember ever saying a dozen words to him. He's got a good deal of cheek, whoever he is—and he, and his dinner, and his missing man may all go to

the devil together ! His invitation is absurd !" And
with this ultimatum Mr. Livingstone laid the letter
and envelope neatly together, preparatory to tearing
them into fragments.

But before this purpose was accomplished, another view of the situation came into his mind. "I
don't see why I shouldn't go," he thought. "I've
been muddling all day with this wretched wool man
—which is a bore, even if I have made a pretty good
bargain with him for next season's clip ; and Ned
hasn't come to time, which is another bore, for now
I'll have to eat my dinner alone. And this Dicky
Smith writes like a gentleman, even if he is cheeky ;
and he certainly seems to be in a peck of troubles
about his missing man, and his thirteen at table, and
the rest of it. Why, it's a regular adventure ! And
to think of having an adventure in Philadelphia, of
all places in the world ! By Jove, I'll go !"

V.

"How very, very good of you, Mr. Livingstone,
to come to our rescue !" It was Mrs. Rittenhouse
Smith who spoke, and she spoke in a guarded tone ;
for Livingstone was among the last to arrive, and
she had no desire to publish among her guests the
catastrophe that so nearly had overtaken her.

"And I know," she continued : "that you will understand how sorry I am that this first visit of Mr.
Smith's old friend to our house should be under such

peculiar circumstances. But you will have your reward, for you are to take out the very prettiest and the very brightest girl here. Come and be rewarded!" And Mrs. Smith slipped her hand upon her benefactor's arm, and piloted him across the room.

"Miss Winthrop, permit me to present Mr. Livingstone. Miss Winthrop is half Boston and half European, Mr. Livingstone; and as you, after these ten years abroad, must be wholly European, you can cheer each other as fellow foreigners in the midst of Philadelphia barbarism"—with which pleasant speech the hostess turned quickly to receive the last arrival (a man, of course; only a man would dare to be even near to late at one of Mrs. Rittenhouse Smith's dinners), and then, standing beside the doorway, with Mr. Hutchinson Port, marshalled her company in to dinner. It was a comfort to her to know that for once in his fault-finding life Mr. Port would be compelled, since he was to be seated beside his hostess, to eat his food without abusing it.

Just at this time two things struck Mrs. Smith as odd. One was that as she presented her handsome guest to Miss Grace Winthrop she certainly had felt him start, while his arm had trembled curiously beneath her hand. The other was that as Mr. Rittenhouse Smith left the drawing-room, passing close beside her with Miss Winthrop upon his arm, he made a face at her. The first of these phenomena struck her as curious. The second struck her as ominous. Had it been possible she would have investigated the cause of Mr. Smith's facial demonstration. But it was not possible. She only could breathe a silent prayer that all would go well—and the while sniff anxiously to discover if perchance there were a smell of scorching duck.

Mrs. Smith would have been still more mystified could she have been cognizant at this juncture of her husband's and of Miss Grace Winthrop's and of Mr. Livingstone's thoughts.

The first of these was thinking: "It isn't Van Rensselaer Livingstone, any more than I am; though he certainly looks like him. And I'm sure that he knows that he don't know me. And I think that we've managed to get into a blank idiotic mess!"

And the second of these was thinking : "If he's been in Europe for the past ten years, there's not one chance in fifty that I ever have laid eyes on him. But I know I have !"

And the third of these was thinking: "There isn't a man in the room who looks enough like Dicky Smith to be his tenth cousin. But if ever the goodness of heaven was shown in the affairs of men it is shown here to me to-night !"

VI.

Even as the sun triumphs over the darkness of night and the gloom of the tempest, so did Mrs. Rittenhouse Smith's dinner-party emerge radiantly from the sombre perils which had beset it. It was a brilliant, unqualified success.

Miss Winthrop was good enough to say, when the evening was ended—saying it in that assured, unconscious way that gives to the utterances of Boston people so peculiar a charm—"Really, Mrs. Smith, you have given me not only a delightful dinner, but a delightful surprise; I would not have believed, had I not seen it myself, that outside of Boston so many clever people could be brought together!"

And Mr. Hutchinson Port, upsetting all his traditions, had kept up a running fire of laudatory comment upon the dinner that had filled Mrs. Smith's soul with joy. She had expected him, being cut off by her presence from engaging in his accustomed grumbling, to maintain a moody silence. She had not expected praise : and she valued his praise the more because she knew that he spoke out of the fulness of his wisdom; and because in a matter of such vital moment as eating she knew that she could trust him to be sincere. His only approach to invidious comment was in regard to the terrapin.

With the grave solemnity that marks the serving of this delicacy in Philadelphia; in the midst of a holy calm befitting a sacred rite, the silver vessels were carried around the board, and in hushed rapture (a little puzzling to the Bostonians) the precious mixture was ladled out upon the fourteen plates ; and Mr. Hutchinson Port, as the result of many years of soulful practice, was able to secure to himself at one dexterous scoop more eggs than fell to the lot of any other two men.

It was while rapturously eating these eggs that

he spake: "My dear Mrs. Smith, will you forgive me if I venture to suggest, even to you—for what I have seen this night has convinced me that you are one of the very few people who know what a dinner ought to be—that the Madeira used in dressing terrapin cannot possibly be *too* old?"

VII.

Proceeding in accordance with the cue that Mrs. Smith had given her, Miss Grace Winthrop engaged Mr. Livingstone in conversation upon European topics; and was somewhat astonished to find, in view of his past ten years in Europe, that they evidently had very little interest for him. And all the while that she talked with him she was haunted by the conviction that she had seen him somewhere; and all the while she was aware of something in his manner, she could not tell what, that seemed to imply that she ought to know who he was.

What Miss Grace Winthrop did feel entirely certain about, however, was that this was one of the cleverest and one of the manliest men she had ever come across. His well-shaped hands were big and brown, and his face was brown, and the set of his head and the range of his broad shoulders gave him an alert look and a certain air of command. There was that about him which suggested a vigorous life in the open air. There was nothing to suggest ten years in Europe, unless it were the charm of his manner, and his neat way of saying bright things.

As for Livingstone, he was as one who at the same time is both entranced and inspired. He knew that he never had been happier in his life ; he knew that he never had said so many clever things in so short a time. Therefore it was that these young people always thereafter were most harmoniously agreed that this was the very happiest dinner that they had eaten in all their lives.

It came to an end much too soon for either of them. The ladies left the room, and cigars were invoked to fill their place. This was the moment that Livingstone had looked forward to as affording the first practicable opportunity for taking his host apart and explaining that his, Livingstone's, presence at that particular feast certainly must be owing to some mistake. And this was the moment that Mr. Smith, also, had looked forward to as available for clearing up the mystery—of which his wife still was blissfully ignorant—as to who their stranger guest really was. But the moment now being come, Livingstone weakly but deliberately evaded it by engaging in an animated conversation with Mr. Hutchinson Port in regard to the precise number of minutes and seconds that a duck ought to remain before the fire ; and Mr. Smith—having partaken of his own excellent wines and meats until his whole being was aglow with a benevolent friendliness—contented himself with thinking that, no matter who his guest was, he certainly was a capital fellow ; and that to cross-question him

6

as to his name, at least until the evening was at an end, would be a gross outrage upon the laws of hospitality.

Livingstone, however, had the grace to feel a good deal ashamed of himself as they returned to the drawing-room. In all that had gone before, he had been a victim of circumstances. He had an uncomfortable conviction that his position now was not wholly unlike that of an impostor. But as he pushed aside the portière he beheld a pair of blue eyes which, he flattered himself, betrayed an expression of pleased expectancy—and his compunctions vanished.

There was only a little time left to them, for the evening was almost at an end. Their talk came back to travel. Did she like travelling in America? he asked. Yes, she liked it very much indeed, "only"—as a sudden memory of a past experience flashed into her mind—"one does sometimes meet such dreadfully horrid people!"

They were sitting, as they talked, in a narrow space between a table and the wall, made narrower by the presence of an unused chair. Just as this memory was aroused, some one tried to push by them, and Livingstone, rising, lifted the obstructing chair away. To find a clear space in which to put it down, he lifted it across the table; and for a moment he stood erect, holding the chair out before him at arm's-length.

When he seated himself and turned again to speak to Grace, he was startled to find that her face and shoulders, and even her arms—her arms and shoul-

ders were delectable—were crimson; and in her eyes
he found at last the look of recognition that he had
hoped for earlier in the evening, but that now he had
ceased to expect. Recognition of this emphatic sort
he certainly had not expected at all.

"You — you see," she said, "I al — always have
thought that you were a robber and a murderer, and
shocking things like that. And I didn't really see
you that day, except as you walked away, holding
up that horrid little man, kicking—just as you held
up the chair. Can you ever, ever forgive me for
thinking such wicked things about you, and for being so ungrateful as not to know you at the very
first?"

And Livingstone, then and later, succeeded in con-
vincing her that he could.

VIII.

By an emphatic whisper Miss Grace Winthrop
succeeded in impressing upon her aunt the necessity
—at no matter what sacrifice of the social conven-
tions—of being the last to go. In the matter of
keeping Livingstone, she experienced no difficulty at
all. And when the unnecessary eight had departed,
she presented to her aunt and uncle her deliverer,
and—in a delightfully hesitating way—told to Mr.
and Mrs. Smith the story of her deliverance.

It was when this matter had been explained that
Livingstone, who felt that his position now was ab-

solutely secure, brought up the delicate question of his own identity.

"You can understand, I am sure, Mrs. Smith," he said, "how very grateful I am to you for this evening; but, indeed, I don't think that I am the person you meant to ask. And it has occurred to me, from something that you said about my having been in Europe for a good while, that Mr. Smith might have meant his invitation for Van Rensselaer Livingstone. He's my cousin, you know; and he has spent the last ten years in Europe, and is there yet, I fancy. But I am Van Ruyter Livingstone, and if I can be said to have a home anywhere—except the old home in New York, of course—it is on my sheep range in New Mexico.

"But you won't be cruel enough, Mrs. Smith, after letting me into Paradise—even if I did get in by mistake—to turn me out again; will you?"

And Mrs. Rittenhouse Smith, who was a clever woman, as well as a remarkably clear-sighted one, replied that even if she wanted to turn Mr. Van Ruyter Livingstone out of Paradise she believed that it was now too late.

OUR PIRATE HOARD.

I

My great-great-great-uncle was one of the many sturdy, honest, high-spirited men to whom the early years of the last century gave birth. He was a brave man and a ready fighter, yet was he ever controlled in his actions by so nice a regard for the feelings of others, and through the strong fibre of his hardy nature ran a strain of such almost womanly gentleness and tenderness, that throughout the rather exceptionally wide circle of his acquaintance he was very generally beloved.

By profession he was a pirate, and although it is not becoming in me, perhaps, to speak boastingly of a blood-relation, I would be doing his memory injustice did I not add that he was one of the ablest and most successful pirates of his time. His usual cruising-ground was between the capes of the Chesapeake and the lower end of Long Island; yet now and then, as opportunity offered, he would take a run to the New England coast, and in winter he frequently would drop down to the s'uthard and do a good stroke of business off the Spanish Main. His home station, however, was the Delaware coast, and his family lived in Lewes, being quite the upper crust

of Lewes society as it then was constituted. When
his schooner, the *Martha Ann*, was off duty, she
usually was harbored in Rehoboth Bay. That was
a pretty good harbor for pirate schooners in those
days.

My great-g eat-great-uncle threw himself into his
profession in the hearty fashion that was to be expected from a man of his sincere, earnest character.
He toiled early and late at sea, and on shore he reg-
ulated the affairs of his family so that his expenses
should be well within his large though somewhat
fluctuating income ; and the result of his prudence in
affairs was that he saved the greater portion of what
he earned. The people of Lewes respected him
greatly, and the boys of the town were bidden to
emulate his steady business ways and habit of thrift.
He was, too, a man of public spirit. At his own cost
and charge he renewed the town pump; and he presented the church—he was a very regular church-
goer when on shore—with a large bell of singularly
sweet tone that had come into his possession after a
casual encounter with a Cuban-bound galleon off the
Bahama Banks.

And yet when at last my great-great-great-uncle,
in the fulness of his years and virtues, was gathered
to his fathers, and the sweet-toned Spanish bell tolled
his requiem, everybody was very much surprised to
find that of the fine fortune accumulated during his
successful business career nothing worth speaking of
could be found. The house that he owned in Lewes,
the handsome furniture that it contained, and a sea-

chest in which were some odds and ends of silver-
ware (of a Spanish make) and some few pieces-of-
eight and doubloons, constituted the whole of his
visible wealth.

For my great-great-great-aunt, with a family of
five sons and seven daughters (including three sets
of twins) all under eleven years of age, the outlook
was a sorry one. She was puzzled, too, to think what
had gone with the great fortune which certainly had
existed, and so was everybody else. The explanation that finally was adopted was that my great-
great-great-uncle, in accordance with well established pirate usage, had buried his treasure somewhere,
and had taken the secret of its burial-place with him
to another and a better world. Probability was giv-
en to this conjecture by the fact that he had died in
something of a hurry. He had been brought ashore
by his men after an unexpected (and by him unin-
vited) encounter with a King's ship off the capes of
the Delaware. One of his legs was shot off, and his
head was pretty well laid open by a desperate cutlass
slash. He already was in a raging fever, and although the best medical advice in Lewes was pro-
cured, he died that very night. As he lay dying his
talk was wild and incoherent; but at the very last,
as my great-great-great-aunt well remembered, he
suddenly grew calm, straightened himself in the
bed, and said, with great earnestness: "Sheer up the
plank midway—"

That was all. He did not live to finish the sentence. At the moment, my great-great-great-aunt

believed the words to be nothing more than a delirious use of a professional phrase; and this belief received color from the fact that a little before, in his feverish fancy, he had been capturing a Spanish galleon, and had got about to the part of the affair where the sheering up of a plank midway between the main and mizzen masts, for the accommodation of the Spaniards in leaving their vessel, would be appropriate. Thinking the matter over calmly afterwards, and in the light of subsequent events, she came to the conclusion that he was trying to tell her how and where his treasure was hid. Acting upon this belief, she sheered up all the planks about the house that seemed at all promising. She even had the cellar dug up and the well dragged. But not a scrap of the treasure did she ever find.

And the worst part of it was, that from that time onward our family had no luck at all. Excepting my elderly cousin, Gregory Wilkinson—who inherited a snug little fortune from his mother, and expanded it into a very considerable fortune by building up a large manufacture of carpet-slippers for the export trade—the rule in my family has been a respectable poverty that has just bordered upon actual want. But all the generations since my great-great-great-uncle's time have been cheered, as poverty-stricken people naturally would be cheered, by the knowledge that the pirate hoard was in existence; and by the hope that some day it would be found, and would make them all enormously rich at a jump. From the moment when I first heard of the treasure, as a little boy, I believed in it thoroughly; and I also believed that I was the member of the family destined to discover it.

II.

I was glad to find, when I married Susan, that she believed in my destiny too. After talking the matter over quite seriously, we decided that the best thing for us to do was to go and live either in or near Lewes, so that my opportunities for investigation might be ample. I think, too, that Susan was pleased with the prospect of having a nice little house of our own, with a cow and peach-trees and chickens, where we could be very happy together. Moreover, she had notions about house-keeping, especially about house-keeping in the country, which she wanted to put into practice.

We found a confirmation of my destiny in the ease with which the preliminaries of my search were accomplished. The house that we wanted seemed to be there just waiting for us — a little bit of a house, well out in the country, with a couple of acres of land around it, the peach-trees really growing, and a shed that the man said would hold a cow nicely. What I think pleased Susan most of all was a swallow's nest under the eaves, with the mother swallow sitting upon a brood of dear little swallows, and the father swallow flying around chippering like anything.

"Just think of it!" said the dear child; "it is like living in a feudal castle, and having kestrels building their nests on the battlements."

I did not check her sweet enthusiasm by asking her to name some particular feudal castle with a frieze of kestrels' nests. I kissed her, and said that it was very like indeed.

Then we examined the cow-stable—we thought it better to call it a cow-stable than a shed—and I pulled out my foot-rule and measured it inside. It was a very little cow-stable, but, as Susan suggested, if we could not get a small grown-up cow to fit it, "we might begin with a young cow, and teach her, as she grew larger, to accommodate herself to her quarters by standing cat-a-cornered, like the man who used to carry oxen up a mountain." Susan's allusions are not always very clearly stated, though her meaning, no doubt, always is quite clear in her own mind. I may mention here that eventually we were so fortunate as to obtain a middle-sized cow that got along in the stable véry well. We had a tidy colored girl who did the cooking and the rough part of the house-work, and who could milk like a steam-engine.

As soon as we got fairly settled in our little home I began to look for my great-great-great-uncle's buried treasure, but I cannot say that at first I made much progress. I could not even find a trace of my great-great-great-uncle's house in Lewes, and nobody seemed ever to have heard of him. One day, though, I was so fortunate as to encounter a very

old man—known generally about Lewes as Old Jacob—who did remember " the old pirate," as he ir-
reverently called him, and who showed me where his
house had been. The house had burned down when
he was a boy—seventy years back, he thought it was
—and across where it once had stood a street had
been opened. This put a stop to my search in that
direction. As Susan very justly observed, I could
not reasonably expect the Lewes people to let me
dig up their streets like a gas-piper just on the
chance of finding my family fortune.

I was not very much depressed by this turn of
events, for I was pretty certain in my own mind that
my great-great-great-uncle had not buried his treasure on his own premises. The basis of this belief
was the difficulty—that must have been even greater
in his time—of transporting such heavy substances
as gold and silver across the sandy region between
Lewes and where the *Martha Ann* used to lie at
anchor in Rehoboth Bay. I reasoned that, the bur-
ial being but temporary, my relative would have
been much more likely to have interred his valu-
ables at some point on the land only a short distance from the *Martha Ann's* anchorage. When I
mentioned this theory to Susan she seemed to be
very much impressed by the common-sense of it,
and as I have a great respect for Susan's judgment,
her acquiescence in my views strengthened my own
faith in them.

To pursue my search in the neighborhood of Rehoboth Bay it was necessary that I should have the

assistance of some person thoroughly familiar with
the coast thereabouts. After thinking the matter
over I decided that I could not do better than take
Old Jacob into my confidence. So I got the old
man out to the Swallow's Nest—that was the name
that Susan had given our country place : only by the
time that she had settled upon it the little swallows
had grown up and the whole swallow family had
gone away—under pretence of seeing if the cow
was all right (Old Jacob was a first-rate hand at
cow doctoring), and while he was looking at the cow
I told him all about the buried treasure, and how I
wanted him to help me find it. When I put it in
his head this way he remembered perfectly the story
that used to be told about the old pirate's mysteri-
ously lost fortune, and he entered with a good deal
of spirit into my project for getting it again. Of
course I told him that if we did find it he should
have a good slice of it for helping me. I told Susan
that I had made this promise, and she said that I had
done exactly right. So, after we had given him a
good supper, Old Jacob went back to Lewes, promising that early the next week, after he had got
through a job of boat-painting which he had on hand,
he would go over with me, and we would begin operations on the bay. He seemed to think the case
very promising. He said that when he was only a
tot of a boy his father had pointed out to him the
Martha Ann's anchorage, and that he thought he
could tell to within a cable's length of where the
schooner used to lie. I did not know how long a

cable was, but from the tone in which Old Jacob
spoke of it I judged that it must be short. I felt
very well pleased with the progress that I was making, and when I told Susan all that Old Jacob had
told me, she said that she looked upon the whole matter as being as good as settled. Indeed, she kept me
awake quite a while that night while she sketched the
outlines of the journey in Europe that we would take
as soon as I could get my great-great-great-uncle's
treasure dug up, and its non-interest-bearing doubloons converted into interest-bearing bonds.

III.

The day after I had this talk with Old Jacob I
was rather surprised by getting a telegram from my
cousin Gregory Wilkinson, telling me that he was
coming down to pay us a visit, and would be there
that afternoon. I was not as much astonished as I
would have been if the telegram had come from anybody else, because Gregory Wilkinson had a way of
telegraphing that he was going to do things which
nobody expected him to do, and I was used to it.
Moreover, I had every reason for desiring to maintain very friendly relations with him. He had told
me several times that he had made a will by which
his large fortune was to be divided between me and
a certain Asylum for the Relief and Education of
Destitute Red Indian Children that he was very much

interested in; and he had more than hinted that the
asylum was not the legatee that was the more to be
envied. This made me feel quite comfortable about
the remote future, but it did not simplify the prob-
lem of living comfortably in the immediate present.
My cousin was a very tough, wiry little man, barely turned of fifty. There was any quantity of life
left in him—his father, who had been just such another, had lived till he was eighty-nine. There was
not much of a chance, therefore, that either the asylum or I would receive anything from his estate for
ever so long—and I may add I was very glad, for
my part, that things were that way. Gregory Wilkinson was a first-rate fellow, for all his queerness
and sudden ways, and I should have been sorry
enough to have been his chief heir. One reason why
I liked him so much was because he was so fond of
Susan. When we were married—although he had
not seen her then — he sent her forks, and he had
lived up to those forks ever since.

Susan was rather flustered when I showed her the
telegram; but she went to work with a will, and got
the little spare room in order, and stewed some
peaches and made some biscuits for supper. Susan's
biscuits were something extraordinary. Gregory
Wilkinson came all right, and after supper—he said
that it was the nicest supper he had eaten in a long
while—she did the honors of the Swallow's Nest in
the pretty way that is her especial peculiarity. She
showed him the cow-stable, with the cow in it, and
the colored girl milking away in her usual vigorous

fashion, the chickens, the garden, the peach-trees, and the nest under the eaves where the swallows had lived when we first came there. Then, as it grew dark, we sat on the little veranda while we smoked our cigars—that is, Gregory Wilkinson and I smoked: all that Susan did was to try to poke her finger through the rings which I blew towards her—and I told why we had come down there, and what a good start we had made towards finding my great-great-great-uncle's buried money. And when I had got through, Susan told how, as soon as I had found it, we were going to Europe.

We neither of us thought that Gregory Wilkinson manifested as much enthusiasm in the matter as the circumstances of the case demanded; but then, as Susan pointed out to me, in her usual clear-headed way, it was not reasonable to expect a man with a fortune to be as eager to get one as a man without one would be.

"Very likely he'll give us his share for finding it," said Susan; "he don't want it himself, and it would be dreadful to turn the heads of all those destitute red Indian children by leaving it to them."

I should have mentioned earlier that, so far as we knew, my cousin and I were my great-great-great-uncle's only surviving heirs. The family luck had not held out any especially strong temptations in the way of pleasant things to live for, and so the family gradually had died off. Whatever my search should bring to light, therefore, would be divided between us two.

7

By the time that Old Jacob got through with his boat-painting, Gregory Wilkinson had gathered a sufficient interest in our money-digging to volunteer to go along with us to the bay. We had a two-seated wagon, and I took with me several things which I thought might be useful in an expedition of this nature — two spades, a pickaxe, a crow-bar, a measuring tape that belonged to Susan, an axe, and a lantern (for, as Susan very truly said, we might have to do some of our digging after dark). I took also a pulley and a coil of rope, in case the box of treasure should prove so heavy that we could not otherwise pull it out from the hole. Old Jacob knew all about rigging tackle, and said that we could cut a pair of sheer-poles in the woods. We were very much encouraged by the confident way in which Old Jacob talked about cutting sheer-poles; it sounded wonderfully business-like. Susan, of course, was very desirous of going along, and I very much wanted to take her. But as we intended to stay all night, in case we did not find the treasure during our first day's search, and as the only place where we could sleep was an oysterman's shanty that Old Jacob knew about, she saw herself that it would not do. So she made the best of staying at home, in her usual cheery fashion, and promised, as we drove off, to have a famous supper ready for us the next night — when we would come home with our wagon-load of silver and gold.

It was a long, hot, dusty drive, and the mosquitoes were pretty bad as we drew near the coast. But we

were cheered by the thought of the fortune that was
so nearly ours, and we smoked our pipes at the mosquitoes in a way that astonished them. After we
had taken out the horses and had eaten our dinner
(Susan had put us up a great basket of provisions,
with two of her own delicious peach pies on top) we
walked down to the bay-side, with Old Jacob leading, to look for the place where the *Martha Ann*
used to anchor. I took the tape-measure along, both
because it might be useful, and because it made me
think of Susan.

I was sorry to find that the clearer the lay of the
land and water became, the more indistinct grew
Old Jacob's remembrance of where his father had
told him that the schooner used to lie.

"It mought hev ben about here," he said, pointing across to a little bay some way off on our left;
"an' agin it mought hev ben about thar," with a
wave of his hand towards a low point of land nearly
half a mile off on our right; "an' agin it mought
hev ben sorter atwixt an' atween 'em. Here or hereabouts, thet's w'at I say; here or hereabouts, sure."

Now this was perplexing. My plan, based upon
Old Jacob's assurance that he could locate the anchorage precisely, was to hunt near the shore for
likely-looking places and dig them up, one after another, until we found the treasure. But to dig up
all the places where treasure might be buried along
a whole mile of coast was not to be thought of. We
implored Old Jacob to brush up his memory, to look
attentively at the shape of the coast, and to try to

fix definitely the spot off which the schooner had
lain. But the more that he tried, the more confusing did his statements become. Just as he would
settle positively — after much thinking and much
looking at the sun and the coast line—on a particular spot, doubts would arise in his mind as to the
correctness of his location ; and these doubts presently would resolve themselves into the certainty
that he was all wrong. Then the process of thinking and looking would begin all over again, only
again to come to the same disheartening end. The
short and long of the matter was that we spent all
that day and a good part of the next in wandering
along the bay - side in Old Jacob's wake, while he
made and unmade his locations at the rate of about
three an hour. At last I looked at Gregory Wilkinson and Gregory Wilkinson looked at me, and we
both nodded. Then we told Old Jacob that we
guessed we'd better hitch up the horses and drive
home. It made us pretty dismal, after all our hopes,
to hitch up the horses and drive home that way.

My heart ached when I saw Susan leaning over
the front gate watching for us as we drove up the
road. The wind was setting down towards us, and
I could smell the coffee that she had put on the fire
to boil as soon as she caught sight of us—Susan
made coffee splendidly—and I knew that she had
kept her promise, and had ready the feast that was
to celebrate our success ; and that made it all the
dismaller that we hadn't any success to celebrate.

When I told her how badly the expedition had

turned out she came very near crying; but she gave a sort of gulp, and then laughed instead, and did what she could to make things pleasant for us. We had our feast, but notwithstanding Susan's effort to be cheerful, it was about as dreary a feast as I ever had anything to do with. We brought Old Jacob in and let him feast with us; and he, to do him justice, was not dreary at all. He seemed to enjoy it thoroughly. Indeed, the most trying part of that sorrowful supper-party was the way in which Old Jacob recovered his spirits and declared at short intervals that his memory now was all right again. He even went so far as to say that with his eyes blindfolded and in the dark he could lead us to the precise spot off which the schooner used to lie.

Susan was disposed to regard these assertions hopefully; but we, who had been fumbling about with him for two days, well understood their baselessness. It was not Old Jacob's fault, of course, but his defective memory certainly was dreadfully provoking. Here was an enormous fortune slipping through our fingers just because this old man could not remember a little matter about where a schooner had been anchored.

After he had eaten all the supper that he could hold—which was a good deal—and had gone home, we told Susan the whole dismal story of how our expedition had proved to be a total failure. It was best, we thought, not to mince matters with her; and we stated minutely how time after time the anchorage of the schooner had been precisely located,

and then in a little while had been unlocated again.
She saw, as we did, that as a clew Old Jacob was
not much of a success, and also that he was about
the only thing in the least like a clew that we possessed. Realizing this latter fact, and knowing that
his great age made his death probable at any moment, Susan strongly advised me, in her clear-sighted way, to have him photographed.

IV.

Gregory Wilkinson seemed to find himself quite
comfortable in our little home, and settled down
there into a sort of permanency. We were glad to
have him stay with us, for he was a first-rate fellow,
and always good company in his pleasant, quiet way,
and he told us two or three times that he was enjoying himself. He told me a great many more than
two or three times that he considered Susan to be a
wonderfully fine woman ; indeed, he told me this at
least once every day, and sometimes oftener. He
was greatly struck—just as everybody is who lives
for any length of time in the same house with Susan
—by her capable ways, and by her unfailing equanimity and sweetness of temper. Even when the
colored girl fell down the well, carrying the rope
and the bucket along with her, Susan was not a bit
flustered. She told me just where I would find the
clothes-line and a big meat-hook ; and when, with

this hastily-improvised apparatus, we had fished the
colored girl up and got her safely on dry land again,
she knew exactly what to do to make her all right
and comfortable. As Gregory Wilkinson observed
to me, after it was all over, from the way that Susan
behaved, any one might have thought that hooking
colored girls up out of wells was her regular business.

As to making Susan angry, that simply was impossible. When things went desperately wrong with
her in any way she would just come right to me and
cry a little on my shoulder. Then, when I had comforted her, she would chipper up and be all right
again in no time. Gregory Wilkinson happened to
come in one day while a performance of this sort
was going on, and for fear that he should think it
odd Susan explained to him that it was a habit of
hers when things very much worried her and she felt
like being ugly to people. (The trouble that day
was that the colored girl, who had a wonderful faculty for stirring up tribulation, had broken an India
china teacup that had belonged to Susan's grand-
mother, and that Susan had thought the world of.)
That evening, while we were sitting on the veranda
smoking, and before Susan, who was helping clear
the supper-table, had joined us, Gregory Wilkinson
said to me, with even more emphasis than usual,
that Susan was the finest woman he had ever known ;
and he added that he was very sorry that when he
was my age he had not met and married just such
another.

He and I talked a good deal at odd times about the money that our great-great-great-uncle the pirate had buried, and that through all these years had stayed buried so persistently. He did not take much interest in the matter personally, but for my sake, and still more for Susan's sake, he was beginning to be quite anxious that the money should be found. He even suggested that we should take Old Jacob over to the bay-side and let him try again to find the *Martha Ann's* anchorage; but a little talk convinced us that this would be useless. The old man had been given every opportunity, during the two days that we had cruised about with him, to refresh his memory; and we both had been the pained witnesses of the curious psychological fact that the more he refreshed it, the more utterly unmanageable it had become. The prospect, we agreed, was a disheartening one, for it was quite evident that for our purposes Old Jacob was, as it were, but an elderly, broken reed.

About this time I noticed that Gregory Wilkinson was unusually silent, and seemed to be thinking a great deal about something. At first we were afraid that he was not quite well, and Susan offered him both her prepared mustard plasters and her headache powders. But he said that he was all right, though he was very much obliged to her. Still, he kept on thinking, and he was so silent and preoccupied that Susan and I were very uncomfortable. To have him around that way, and to be always wondering what he could possibly be thinking about, Susan said, made her feel as though she were trying to eavesdrop when nobody was talking.

One afternoon while we were sitting on the veranda—Susan and I trying to keep up some sort of a conversation, and Gregory Wilkinson thinking away as hard as ever he could think — a thin man in a buggy drove down the road and stopped at our hitching-post. When he had hitched his horse he took out from the after-part of the buggy a large tin vessel standing on light iron legs, and came up to the house with it. He made us all a sort of comprehensive bow, but stopped in front of Susan, set the tin vessel upon its legs, and said :

"Madam, you behold before you the most economical device and the greatest labor-saving invention of this extraordinarily devicious and richly inventive age. This article, madam"—and he placed his hand upon the tin vessel affectionately—"is Stowe's patent combination interchangeable churn and washboiler."

Susan did not say anything; she simply shuddered.

"As at present arranged, madam," the man went on, "it is a churn. Standing thus upon these light yet firm legs" (the thing wobbled outrageously), "with this serviceable handle projecting from the top, and communicating with an exceptionally effective churning apparatus within, it is beyond all doubt the very best churn, as well as the cheapest, now offered on the American market. But observe, madam, that as a wash-boiler it is not less excellent.

By the simple process of removing the handle, taking out the dasher, and unshipping the legs — the work, as you perceive, of but a moment—the process of transformation is complete. As to the trifling orifice that the removal of the handle leaves in the lid, it becomes, when the wash-boiler side of this Protean vessel is uppermost, a positive benefit. It is an effective safety-valve. Without it, I am not prepared to say that the boiler would not burst, scattering around it the scalded, mangled remains of your washer-woman and utterly ruining your week's wash.

"And mark, madam, mark most of all, the economy of this invention. I need not say to you, a housekeeper of knowledge and experience, that churning-day and wash-day stand separate and distinct upon your household calendar. Under no circumstances is it conceivable that the churn and the wash-boiler shall be required for use upon the same day. Clearly the use of the one presupposes and compels the neglect of the other. Then why cumber your house with these two articles, equally large and equally unwieldly, when, by means of the beautiful invention that I have the honor of presenting to your notice, the two in one can be united, and money and house-room alike can be saved? I trust, madam, I believe, that I have said enough to convince you that my article is all that fancy can paint or bright hope inspire; that in every household made glad by its presence it will be regarded always and forever as a heaven-given boon!" Suddenly dropping his rhetorical tone and coming down to the tone of business, the man went on : "You'll buy one, won't you? The price—"

The change of tone seemed to arouse Susan from the spellbound condition in which she had remained during this extraordinary harangue.

" O-o-o-oh !" she said, shudderingly, "do take the horrid, horrid thing right away !" Then she fled into the house.

I was very angry at the man for disturbing Susan in this way, and I told him so pretty plainly ; and I also told him to get out. At this juncture, to my astonishment, Gregory Wilkinson interposed by asking what the thing was worth ; and when the man said five dollars, he said that he would buy it. The man had manifested a disposition to be ugly while I was giving him his talking to, but when he found that he had made a sale, after all, he grew civil again. As he went off he expressed the hope that the lady would be all right presently, and the conviction that she would find the combination churn and wash-boiler a household blessing that probably would add ten years to her life.

" What on earth did you buy that for ?" I asked, when the man had gone.

" Oh, I don't know. It seems to be a pretty good wash - boiler, anyway. I heard your wife say the other day that she wanted a wash - boiler. She needn't use it as a churn if she don't want to, you know."

" But my wife never will tolerate that disgusting

thing, with its horrid suggestiveness of worse than Irish uncleanliness, about the house," I went on, rather hotly. "I really must beg of you to send it away."

"All right," he answered. "I'll *take* it away. I'm going to New York to-morrow, and I'll take it along."

"And what ever will you do with it in New York?" I asked.

"Well, I can't say positively yet, but I guess I'll send it out to the asylum. They'd be glad to get it there, I don't doubt—not as a churn, you know, but for wash-boiling."

Then he went on to tell me that one of the things that he especially wanted done at the asylum with his legacy was the construction of a steam-laundry, with a thing in the middle that went round and round, and dried the clothes by centrifugal pressure. He explained that the asylum was only just starting as an asylum, and was provided not only with very few destitute red Indian children, but also with very few of the appliances which an institution of that sort requires, and that was the reason why he had selected it, in preference to many other very deserving charities, to leave his money to.

I must say that I was glad to hear him talking in this strain, for his sudden announcement of his intended departure for New York, just after I had spoken so warmly to him, made me fear that I had offended him. But it was clear that I hadn't, and that his going off in this unexpected fashion did not

mean anything. He always did have a fancy for
doing things suddenly.

Susan was worried about it, in just the same way,
when I told her ; but she ended by agreeing with me
that he was not in the least offended at anything. Indeed, that evening we both were very much pleased
to notice what good spirits he was in. His preoccupied manner was entirely gone, and, for him, he was
positively lively. Evidently, whatever the thing was
that he had been thinking about so hard, he had
settled it in a way that satisfied him.

Just as we were going to bed he told me, in what
struck me at the time as rather an odd tone, that he
was under the impression that he had somewhere a
chest full of old family papers, and that possibly
among these papers there might be something that
would tell me how to find the fortune that Susan
and I certainly deserved to have. As he said this
he laughed in a queer sort of way, and then he
looked at Susan very affectionately, and then he
took each of us by the hand.

"Oh !" said Susan, rapturously (when Susan is ex-
cited she always begins what she has to say with an
"Oh !" I like it). "To think of finding a piece of
old yellow parchment with a quite undecipherable
cryptogram written on it in invisible ink telling us
just where we ought to dig ! How perfectly lovely !
Why *didn't* you think of it sooner ?"

"Because I have been neither more nor less than
a blind old fool. And—and I have to thank you,
my dear," he continued, still speaking in the queer

tone, " for having effectually opened my eyes." As he made this self-derogatory and quite incomprehensible statement he turned to Susan, kissed her in a great hurry, shook our hands warmly, said goodnight, and trotted off up-stairs to his room. His conduct was very extraordinary. But then, as I have already mentioned, Gregory Wilkinson had a way of always doing just the things which nobody expected him to do.

He had settled back into his ordinary manner by morning ; at least he was not much queerer than usual, and bade us good-bye cheerily at the Lewes railway station. I had hired a light wagon and had driven him over in time for the early train, bringing Susan along, so that she might see the last of him. What with all three of us, his trunk and valise, and the churn-wash-boiler, we had a wagon-load.

Susan was horrified at the thought of his giving the churn-wash-boiler to the asylum. " Even if they only are allowed to use it as a wash-boiler," she argued, earnestly, " think what dreadful ideas of untidiness it will put into those destitute red Indian children's heads !—ideas," she went on, " which will only tend to make them disgrace instead of doing credit to the position of easy affluence to which your legacy will lift them when they return to their barbaric wilds. If you *must* give it to them, at least conceal from them — I beg of you, conceal from them—the fatal fact that it ever was meant to be a churn too."

Gregory Wilkinson promised Susan that he would conceal this fact from the destitute red Indian children ; and then the train started, and he and the churn-wash-boiler were whisked away. We really were very sorry to part with him.

V.

Two or three days later I happened to meet Old Jacob as I was coming away from the post-office in Lewes, and I was both pained and surprised to perceive that the old man was partially intoxicated. When he caught sight of me he came at me with such a lurch that had I not caught him by the arm he certainly would have fallen to the ground. At first he resented this friendly act on my part, but in a moment he forgot his anger and insisted upon shaking hands with me with most energetic warmth. Then he swayed his lips up to my ear, and asked in a hoarse whisper if that old cousin chap of mine had got home safely the night before; and wanted to know, with a most mysterious wink, if things was all right *now*.

I was grieved at finding Old Jacob in this unseemly condition, and I also was ruffled by his very rude reference to my cousin. I endeavored to disengage my hand from his, and replied with some dignity that Mr. Wilkinson at present was in New York, whither he had returned several days previously. But Old Jacob declined to relinquish my hand, and, with more mysterious winks, declared in a muzzy voice that I might trust *him*, and that I needn't say that my cousin was in New York, when he and him had been a-ridin' around together to the bay and back ag'in only the day before. And then he went off into a rambling account of this expedition, which in its main features resembled the expedition that we all three had taken together, but which displayed certain curious details as it advanced that I could not at all account for. By all odds the most curious of these details was that they had taken along with them a large tin vessel, Old Jacob's description of which tallied strangely closely with that of the churn-wash-boiler, and that they had left it behind them when they returned. But as he mixed this up with a lot of stuff about having shown my cousin the course of an old creek that a storm had filled with sand fifty years and more before, I could not make head nor tail of it.

Yet somehow there really did seem to be more than mere drunken fancy in what he was telling me; for in spite of his muzzy way of telling it, his story had about it a curious air of truth; and yet it all was so utterly preposterous that belief in it was quite out of the question. To make matters worse, when I begged the old man to try to remember very carefully whether or not he really had made a second trip to the bay, or only was telling me about the trip that the three of us had made together, he suddenly got very angry, and said that he supposed I thought he was drunk, and if anybody was drunk I was, and he'd fight me for five cents any time. And then he began to shake his old fists at me, and to go on in such a boisterous way that, in order to avoid a very unpleasant scene upon the public streets, I had to leave him and come home.

When I told Susan the queer story that Old Jacob had told me she was as much perplexed and disturbed by it as I was. To think of Gregory Wilkinson driving around the lower part of the State of Delaware in this secret sort of way, in company with Old Jacob and the churn-wash-boiler, as she very truly said, was like a horrible dream ; and she asked me to pinch her to make sure that it wasn't.

"But even pinching me don't prove anything," she said, when I had performed that office for her. "For—don't you see?—I might dream that I was dreaming, and asked you to pinch me, and that you did it; and I suppose," she went on, meditatively, "that I might even dream that I woke up when you pinched me, and yet that I might be sound asleep all the while. It really is dreadfully confusing, when you come to think of it, this way in which you can have dreams inside of each other, like little Chinese boxes, and never truly know whether you're asleep or awake. I don't like it at all."

Without meaning to, Susan frequently talks quite in the manner of a German metaphysician.

The next day we recived a letter from Gregory Wilkinson that we hoped, as we opened it, would clear up the mystery. But before we had finished

8

it we were in such a state of excitement that we
quite forgot that there was any mystery to clear
up. My cousin wrote from his home in New York,
and made no allusion whatever to a second visit
to Lewes, still less to a second expedition with Old
Jacob to Rehoboth Bay. After speaking very nicely
of the pleasant time that he had passed with us, he
continued :

"I enclose a memorandum that seems to have a
bearing upon the whereabouts of the hidden family
fortune. I am sorry, for Susan's sake, that it is
neither invisible nor undecipherable ; but I think
that for practical purposes visible ink and readable
English are more useful. I advise you to attend to
the matter at once. It may rain."

The enclosure was a scrap of paper, so brown with
age that it looked as though it had been dipped in
coffee, on which was written, in astonishingly black
ink, this brief but clear direction :

*Sheer uppe ye planke midwai atween ye oake and
ye hiccorie saplyngs 7 fathom Est of Pequinky crik
on ye baye. Ytte is all there.*

There was no date, no signature, to this paper, but
neither Susan nor I doubted for a moment that it
was the clew to my great-great-great-uncle's missing
fortune. With a heart almost too full for utterance,
Susan went straight across the room to the big dictionary (Gregory Wilkinson had given it to us at
Christmas, with a handy iron stand to keep in on),
and in a trembling voice the dear child told me in
one single breath that a fathom was a measure of

length containing six feet or two yards, generally used in ascertaining the depth of the sea. Then, without waiting to close the dictionary, she threw herself into my arms and asked me to kiss her hard !

Susan wanted to start right off that afternoon— she was determined to go with me this time, and I had not the heart to refuse her; but I represented to her that night would be upon us before we could get across to the bay, and that we had better wait till morning. But I at once went over and hired the light wagon for the next day, and then we got together the things which we deemed necessary for the expedition. The tape-measure, of course, was a most essential part of the outfit. Susan declared that she would take exclusive charge of that herself ; it made her feel that she was of importance, she said. During all the evening she was quite quivering with excitement—and so was I, for that matter—and I don't believe that we slept forty winks apiece all night long.

We were up bright and early, and got off before seven o'clock—after Susan had given the colored girl a great many directions as to what she should and should not do while we were gone. This was the first time that we ever had left the colored girl alone in the house for a whole day, and Susan could not help feeling rather anxious about her. It would be dreadful, she said, to come home at night and find her bobbing up and down dead at the bottom of the well.

As we drew near the bay I asked several people

whom we happened to meet along the road if they knew where Pequinky Creek was, and I was rather surprised to find that they all said they didn't. At last, however, we were so fortunate as to meet with quite an old man who was able to direct us. He seemed to be a good deal astonished when I put the question to him, but he answered, readily :

"Yes, yes, o' course I knows where 'tis — 'tain't nowhere. Why, young man, there hain't ben any Pequinky Crik fur th' better part o' sixty year— not sence thet gret May storm druv th' bay shore right up on eend an' dammed th' crik short off, an' turned all th' medders thereabouts inter a gret nasty ma'sh, an' med a new outlet five mile an' more away t' th' west'ard. Not a sign o' Pequinky Crik will you find at this day—an' w'at I should like ter know is w'ere on yeth a young feller like you ever s' much as heerd tell about it."

This was something that I had not counted on, and I could see that Susan was feeling very low in her mind. But by questioning the old man closely I gradually got a pretty clear notion of where the mouth of the creek used to be ; and I concluded that, unless the oak and hickory had been cut down or washed away, I stood a pretty good chance of finding the spot that I was in search of. Susan did not take this hopeful view of the situation. She was very melancholy.

Following the old man's directions, I drove down to the point on the road that was nearest to where the Pequinky in former times had emptied into the bay; then I hitched the horse to a tree, and with Susan and the tape-measure began my explorations. They lasted scarcely five minutes. With no trouble at all I found the oak and the hickory—grown to be great trees, as I had expected—and with the tape-measure we fixed the point midway between them in no time. Then I went back to the wagon for the spade and the other things, Susan going along and dancing around and around me in sheer delight. It is a fortunate trait of Susan's character that while her spirits sometimes do fall a very long distance in a very short time, they rise to proportionate heights with proportionate rapidity.

The point that we had fixed between the trees was covered thickly with leaves, and when I had cleared these away and had begun to dig, I was surprised to find that the soil came up freely, and was not matted together with roots as wood soil ought to be. I should have paid more attention to this curious fact, no doubt, had I not been so profoundly stirred by the excitement incident to the strange work in which I was engaged. As for Susan, the dear creature said that she had creeps all over her, for she knew that the old pirate's ghost must be hovering near, and she begged me to notify her when I came to the skeleton, so that she might look away. I told her that I did not expect to find a skeleton, but she replied that this only showed how ignorant *I* was of pirate ceremonial; that it was the rule with all pirates when burying treasure to sacrifice a human life, and to bury the dead body

over the hidden gold.   She admitted, however—
upon my drawing her attention to the fact that the
treasure which we were in the act of digging up
had been placed here by my relative only for temporary security—that in this particular instance the
human sacrifice part of the pirate programme might
have been omitted.

J ust as we had reached this conclusion—which disappointed Susan a little, I think—my spade struck
with a heavy thud against a piece of wood.   Clearing the earth away, I disclosed some fragments of
rotten plank, and beneath these I saw something
that glittered !   Susan, standing beside me on the
edge of the hole, saw the glitter too.   She did not
say one word ; she simply put both her arms around
my neck and kissed me.

I rapidly removed the loose earth, and then with
the pickaxe I heaved the plank up bodily.   But
what we saw when the plank came away was not a
chest full of doubloons, pieces-of-eight, moidores, and
other such ancient coins, mingled with golden orna-
ments thickly studded with precious stones ; no, we
saw the very bright lid of a tin box, a circular box,
rather more than two feet in diameter.   There was
a small round hole in the centre of the lid, into which
a little roll of newspaper was stuffed—presumably
to keep the sand out—and beside this hole I noticed,
soldered fast to the lid, a small brass plate on which
my eye caught the word "Patented."   It was strange
enough to find the tin box in such perfect preserva-
tion while the stout oak plank above it had rotted

into fragments; but the wisp of newspaper, and the brass plate with its utterly out-of-place inscription, were absolutely bewildering. My head seemed to be going around on my shoulders, while something inside of it was buzzing dreadfully. Suddenly Susan exclaimed, in a tone of disgust and consternation: "It's—it's that perfectly horrid churn-wash-boiler!"

As she spoke these doomful words I recalled Old Jacob's drunken story, which I now perceived must have been true, and the dreadful thought flashed into my mind that Gregory Wilkinson must have gone crazy, and that this dreary practical joke was the first result of his madness. Susan meanwhile had sunk down by the side of the hole and was weeping silently.

As a vent to my outraged feelings I gave the wretched tin vessel a tremendous poke with the spade, that caved in one side of it and knocked the lid off. I then perceived that within it was an ob-long package carefully tied up in oiled silk, and on bending down to examine the package more closely I perceived that it was directed to Susan. With a dogged resolve to follow out Gregory Wilkinson's hideous pleasantry to the bitter end, I lifted the package out of the box—it was pretty heavy—and began to open it. Inside the first roll of the cover was a letter that also was directed to Susan. She had got up by this time, and read it over my shoulder.

"MY DEAR SUSAN,—I have decided not to wait until I die to do what little good I can do in the world.   You will be glad, I am sure, to learn that I have made arrangements for the immediate erection of the steam-laundry at the asylum, as well as for the material improvement in several other ways of that excellent institution.

"At the same time I desire that you and your husband shall have the benefit immediately of the larger portion of the legacy that I always have intended should be yours at my death.   It is here (in govt. 4's), and I hope with all my heart that your trip to Europe will be a pleasant one.   I am very affectionately yours,   GREGORY WILKINSON."

"And to think," said Susan—as we drove home through the twilight, bearing our sheaves with us and feeling very happy over them—"and to think that it should turn out to be your cousin Gregory Wilkinson who was the family pirate and had a hoard, and not your great-great-great-uncle, after all!"

A TEMPORARY DEAD-LOCK.

I.

Mr. John Amesbury, Senior Warden of St. Jude's Church, Minneapolis, to the Rev. Clement Markham :

VESTRY OF ST. JUDE'S, *April 4th.*

DEAR MR. MARKHAM,—At a special meeting of the wardens and vestry of St. Jude's Church held this day, it was unanimously decided to grant your request for leave of absence from your duties as rector of this parish from June 1st till September 13th, inclusive, proximo, with permission to go abroad. I am instructed further to state that the wardens and vestry of St. Jude's have much pleasure in granting your request, as they feel that your zealous and very successful administration of the affairs of the parish has abundantly entitled you to a period of relaxation and rest. Your salary for the term of your absence will be paid to you in advance.

In my personal capacity, my dear Markham, permit me to add that I am delighted that you are to have this holiday. You richly deserve it. By-the-way, a good deal of amusement was caused by the rather characteristic error in the date of your formal application for leave. Were you to receive precisely

the holiday that you asked for, you would have to
turn back the wheels of time, for your letter was
dated *last year!*

II.

Mrs. Clement Markham to Mrs. Winthrop Tremont,
Boston:

St. Jude's Rectory, Minneapolis, *May 15th.*

DEAR AUNT LUCY,—We are getting on famously
with our preparations for the summer. Dear Clement is full of his visit to England, and I am sure
that he will have a delightful time. The bishop has
given him a letter of introduction to the Bishop
of London, and another to Dean Rumford, of Can-
terbury, so a very desirable introduction to the best
clerical society is assured to him. He expects to sail
from New York on the *City of Paris* June 5th, and
to sail from London on the same vessel on September 4th. This will bring him back to New York in
plenty of time to get home to preach on the next
Sunday, the 14th. He expects to write his sermon
on the voyage. It would be delightful to go with
him, but this is impossible on account of the children. I have engaged board for the summer at a
small but very good hotel in the White Mountains
—the Outlook House, Littleton, New Hampshire—
and I expect to be very comfortable there. I made
a funny mistake in writing for my rooms. I directed
my first letter to Littleton, *New York.* Wasn't it
absurd?

Dear Clement expects to get some vestments in London, where they make them so well, you know, and he has promised to bring me from Paris—where he will spend a fortnight—two dozen pairs of gloves and six pairs of black silk stockings.   Fancy my having six pairs of black silk stockings at once!   I shall feel like a queen.   The children are very well.

III.

The Rev. Clement Markham to Mrs. Clement Markham, Littleton, New Hampshire:

ON BOARD "CITY OF PARIS," *June 5th*—3:30 P.M.

. . . I stayed with my brother Ronald last night, and he and Van Cortlandt came down to see me off. I barely caught the steamer, for I forgot my watch —left it on the mantel-piece in Ronald's chambers— and did not remember it until we were half-way down town.   Ronald said, in his chaffing way, that I left my head somewhere when I was a boy, and that I have been going around without it ever since. I wish that he and Van Cortlandt hadn't such silly notions about my incapacity in the ordinary affairs of life—not that I really mind their nonsense, for you know how well I love them both.   I am very glad that you consented to go directly to the mountains instead of coming to New York to see me off. There was a great crowd on the dock, and I much prefer to think of our tender parting. . . . Be sure to

cable me on the 15th—the day that I get to London.
The address, you know, is simply, "Clement, London," and I am to arrange with my bankers to have
the despatch sent to me.   Good-bye, my—   Here is
the pilot.

IV.

The Rev. Clement Markham to Mrs. Clement Markham, Littleton, New Hampshire :

[*Cable Despatch.*]

LONDON, *June 16th.*

Why have you not cabled ?

V.

The Rev. Clement Markham to Mrs. Clement Markham, Littleton, New Hampshire :

CHARING CROSS HOTEL, LONDON, *June 16th.*

. . . After I cabled you this morning I remembered
that I hadn't arranged with the bankers about my
cable despatches.   When I had rectified this error
of omission I received your despatch of yesterday.
It was a very great relief to my mind to have direct
news from you, and to know of the safety and health
of my loved ones, who are dearer to me . . .

VI.

The Rev. Clement Markham to Mrs. Clement Markham, Littleton, New Hampshire:

CHARING CROSS HOTEL, LONDON, *August 20th.*

. . . I had a delightful fortnight in Paris. . . . I bought the gloves and the stockings—it was droll, and not quite proper, about buying the stockings. I will tell you all about it when I get home. And I also bought you Something Else that I am sure will be a pleasant surprise to you when you see it. . . . His lordship, Dr. ——, has been kindness itself to me. I dined again at Lambeth Palace yesterday— a farewell dinner. I was a little late, I am sorry to say, for I got into the wrong boat at Westminster Bridge, but his lordship very cordially accepted my excuses. At dinner I was seated next to a very interesting man who has charge of a large parish in the east end of London. Such poverty as there is in that wretched region, and such moral depravity, are sickening to contemplate. Thank Heaven, there is nothing like it in Minneapolis. . . .

I shall sail (D. V.) on the *City of Paris* two weeks from to-morrow. I think that the best arrangement will be for you to come down to your aunt Lucy's on the 11th, and on the 12th (D. V.) I will join you at her house in Boston, whence we will start for home that evening *via* the Boston and Al-

bany. I must be in New York for a few hours to
see Ronald and to make the final arrangements about
the new stained-glass windows. If you prefer to
meet me in New York, arrange matters with Ronald,
who will meet you at the station and take you to a
hotel. As I shall go directly to his office on landing,
I will find out at once what you have decided to
do. . . . On referring to your letter of the 10th I
perceive that you are afraid that I may have made
some mistake about the sizes of the stockings and
gloves. Of course I got the right sizes; I had it
written down : "No. 6¼, long fingers," and "No. 8½,
narrow ankles." Don't fall into Ronald's way of
fancying that I always get things wrong. It was
about the narrow ankles that— But I had better
wait and tell it to you when I get home. It certainly was very droll. I have bought a most satisfactory chasuble, very elegant in material and beauti-
fully made. I should have hesitated to buy so costly
a garment for myself ; but this is for the Service of
the Sanctuary. It will make something of a stir
among the congregation, I think, the first time that
I wear it in dear St. Jude's. . . . If, as is probable, I
go down into Wales next week, this will be my last
letter. My heart is full of joyful thankfulness to
think that so very soon I shall see again (D. V.) my
own dear Margaret, who. . . .

VII.

Mrs. Clement Markham to Mrs. Winthrop Tremont, Boston:

LITTLETON, *August 29th.*

DEAR AUNT LUCY,—I have just received a long and delightful letter from dear Clement. He had a lovely time in Paris, and he has bought me the gloves and the silk stockings, and also Something Else; but he won't tell me what this other thing is, for he means it to be a surprise. Do you think it could *possibly* be the silk for a dress? He knows how much I want a new black silk. But I shall not think about it, for I don't want to be disappointed. He has had such delightful dinners with his lordship the Bishop of London at Lambeth Palace. His lordship was "kindness itself," Clement writes. Clement must have made a very favorable impression, of course. And Clement writes that he has bought such a love of a chasuble. It will stir up the whole congregation the first time that he wears it, I am sure.

If it is *quite* convenient to you, dear Aunt Lucy, I shall come down to you, with the nurse and the children, on the 11th. That is the day that Clement will arrive in New York, and he writes that he will come to Boston the next day—after seeing Ronald, and attending to the final arrangements about our beautiful new chancel windows—and join me at your house.

9

But if this arrangement is the *least bit inconvenient* to you, please tell me so frankly, for I can perfectly well meet him in New York, where Ronald will take care of me till he comes — a plan that he also has arranged in case I do not go to you. Dear Clement always is so thoughtful and careful, you know. Please answer soon, so that I may know what to do. The weather is quite chilly here now. The children are brown as little berries and very well. Baby has cut another tooth.

VIII.

Mrs. Winthrop Tremont to Mrs. Clement Markham, Littleton, New Hampshire :

No. 19 MOUNT VERNON PLACE, *August 30th.*

MY DEAR MARGARET,—I write at once because, I am very sorry to say, it will be impossible for me to have you here on the date that you name. I have just completed my arrangements for having the entire house papered and painted. All the furniture is locked up in the dining-room (that was done up, you remember, last summer), and I set out this afternoon on a round of visits that will fill up the time until September 12th, when I am promised that the work will be done. The servants are to have holidays and the painters and paper-hangers are to be in complete possession of the premises. Could I be sure that they would keep their promises and get through by the 12th, I should urge your coming on that day, which still would be in time to meet Clement, instead of on the 11th. But you know how uncertain people of this sort are. Much as I would love to have you and Clement with me, I think that you had better follow out your second plan, and go to Ronald's care in New York.

IX.

Mrs. Clement Markham to Mr. Ronald Markham, New York :

LITTLETON, *August 31st.*

DEAR RONALD,—Clement had arranged, in case we could stay at Aunt Lucy's, to meet me in Boston on his return. But I have just received a letter from Aunt Lucy in which she says that her house is torn up, and that we cannot possibly come to her before the 12th. Therefore I must adopt the other plan that dear Clement, with his usual thoughtfulness, has suggested, which is to meet him in New York. He tells me to ask you to engage rooms for me in some quiet hotel, and also to ask you to meet me on my arrival with the children and nurse. I shall leave here on the morning of the 10th by the White Mountain Express (that gets in at Jersey City, I think) ; and if you will care for me in the way that Clement suggests, I shall be very grateful.

Clement has had a lovely time during his holiday. He has been especially favored by seeing a great deal of the higher clergy. He has dined repeatedly with the Lord Archbishop of London at Lambeth Palace, and I am sure that he must have created a very favorable impression among them, and given them a highly satisfactory idea of the clergymen of the American branch of the Anglican Church. Please answer soon, so that I may know what to do. I forgot to say that Clement expects to arrive on the 11th. He is to sail on the 4th.

X.

The Rev. Clement Markham to Mrs. Clement Markham, Littleton, New Hampshire:

[*Cable Despatch.*]

LIVERPOOL, *September 3d.*

Sail to-day.

XI.

Mr. Ronald Markham to Mrs. Clement Markham, Littleton, New Hampshire:

[*Telegram.*]

SAN ANTONIO, TEXAS, *September 5th.*

Here for a week on railroad business. Van Cortlandt will secure you rooms and meet you. Write him at No. 120 Broadway.

XII.

Mrs. Clement Markham to Mr. Hubert Van Cortlandt, New York:

LITTLETON, *September 5th.*

DEAR MR. VAN CORTLANDT,—By a telegram that I have just received from Ronald, I find that he is in Texas. I had written to him to ask him to secure rooms for me at some quiet hotel, and to meet me at Jersey City on the evening of the 10th, on the arrival of the White Mountain Express. Of course he cannot do this now, and he telegraphs me to ask you to do it all in his place. I feel that I am taking a great liberty in asking so much of you, but I really cannot help myself. I had expected to meet Clement in Boston at my aunt's, but my aunt is out of town; and now Ronald is away from New York. It is very provoking. So, you see, I can only throw myself on your mercy. But I do this with the less hesitation because I know how strong your friendship is for my dear Clement, who will be, as I will be also, very grateful to you.

I am very much puzzled by a cable despatch from Clement that came two days ago. It reads, "Sail to-day," and is dated September *third.* Clement's passage was engaged on the *City of Paris,* which I know was advertised to sail on September *fourth,* and that is the date that he all along has named for his return. Can the date of sailing have been changed?　Ought I to come to New York one day earlier?　Everything seems to be going wrong of late, and I am both worried and perplexed.　If you can think of any comforting explanation that will account for this change, I shall be very much obliged to you.　Please give my kindest regards to Mrs. Van Cortlandt.

XIII.

Mr. Hubert Van Cortlandt to Mrs. Clement Markham, Littleton, New Hampshire :

LAW OFFICES OF

VAN CORTLANDT, HOWARD, WARRINGTON & EDGECOMBE, EQUITABLE BUILDING, 120 BROADWAY.

[*Dictated.*]　　　　　　　　　NEW YORK, *September 7th.*

MY DEAR MRS. MARKHAM,—Your favor of the 5th is received.　I am very glad indeed that I shall have this opportunity to serve you.　You must not consider yourself under any obligation at all.　Remember how close Clement is to me, though our ways in life have separated widely, and how true his friendship has been to me through all these years.　I am delighted that Ronald is out of town, and that I am to be permitted to serve you in his place.

I regret exceedingly that Mrs. Van Cortlandt is still in the Catskills, and that our house still remains in its condition of summer dismantlement.　Were she at home, and the house in order, you would come directly to us, of course.　As this cannot be, I have

engaged an apartment for you with my old land-
lady, Mrs. Warden, No. 68 Clinton Place. For a
number of years before I was married I occupied
rooms in this house, and I am confident that you
will be far more comfortable there than you possibly
could be at any hotel. Mrs. Warden, who is a moth-
erly old body, and who remembers Clement well,
will take the best of care of you, and I have arranged that your meals shall be sent across to you
from the Brevoort.

In regard to Clement's cable despatch, I am as
much puzzled as you are. One of my young men
has just returned from the office of the Inman Line,
and reports that the *City of Paris* sailed on her
regular date, the 4th, and is due to arrive here on
Wednesday next, the 11th. My young man was assured that no steamer belonging to any of the regular lines left Liverpool for this port on the 3d. The
Cunard steamer *Samaria* did leave Liverpool on the
3d, however, for Boston. It is possible, of course—
since your original plan seems to have been that you
and Clement should meet in Boston—that he has
sailed in the *Samaria*. But I do not think that this
is probable. The *Samaria* is a much slower boat
than the *City of Paris*, and I think that even Clement would perceive that by sailing in her he would
lose time instead of gaining it. Frankly, my dear
Mrs. Markham, I think that Clement simply has
mixed things up in his despatch by writing "to-
day" when he meant "to-morrow." Bless his dear
old heart! he always did have a faculty for getting

things wrong, you know. I decidedly advise you, therefore, to come down to New York on the 10th, as you have already arranged.

I observe that you speak of the White Mountain Express as coming in at Jersey City. This is a mistake : it arrives at the Forty-second Street Station. Bear this fact in mind, please ; and I advise you to write on a card—which you had better have easily accessible in your pocket-book—Mrs. Warden's address, No. 68 Clinton Place. Then, should I miss you in the crowd at the station, or should any other mischance occur in regard to our meeting, you will know where to tell your driver to take you, and where to send your trunks. Do not fear that any such untoward accident will occur : it is only professional prudence that leads me to provide for every contingency that may arise. As a further precautionary measure (we lawyers are full of precautionary measures, you know), please telegraph me from Littleton on the morning that you leave.

XIV.

Mrs. Clement Markham to Mr. Hubert Van Cortlandt, New York :

LITTLETON, *September 9th.*

DEAR MR. VAN CORTLANDT, — Your very kind letter came last evening. I cannot tell you how grateful I am to you for all your goodness and thoughtfulness. With such explicit directions I cannot possibly go wrong. You must be right, I think, in regard to the cable despatch. Such a mistake would be just what dear Clement would be almost certain to make when in one of his absent-minded moods. I will do all the prudent things which you so thoughtfully advise, and I shall keep your letter to show to dear Clement, so that he may know how much trouble you have taken to make everything about my arrival secure. Of course, the train does not come in at Jersey City : I remember about it now perfectly. I am in the thick of packing to-day, and expect to get off in the morning ; but I will telegraph you before I start. I don't want to bother you with this letter at your office, so I send it to your house. I find the address in Clement's address-book. Am I not considerate?

XV.

Dr. Atwood Vance to Mr. Hubert Van Cortlandt, New York :

[*Telegram.*]

TANNERSVILLE, NEW YORK, *September 9th.*

Mrs. Van Cortlandt taken dangerously ill in night, and continues in critical condition. Come at once.

XVI.

Mrs. Clement Markham to Mr. Hubert Van Cortlandt, New York:

[*Telegram. Endorsed: "Not delivered. Party out of town."*]

LITTLETON, NEW HAMPSHIRE, *September 10th.*

Will arrive on White Mountain Express this evening.

XVII.

The Rev. Clement Markham to Mrs. Clement Markham, No. 19 Mount Vernon Place, Boston:

[*Telegram. Endorsed: "Returned to sender. Unknown at this address."*]

BREVOORT HOUSE, NEW YORK, *September 11th.*

Arrived this morning.   Will be with you (D. V.) to-morrow.

XVIII.

The Rev. Clement Markham to Mrs. Winthrop Tremont, No. 19 Mount Vernon Place, Boston:

[*Telegram. Endorsed: "Returned to sender. Addressee absent from Boston."*]

BREVOORT HOUSE, NEW YORK, *September 11th.*

Is Margaret with you ?   Please answer at once.

XIX.

The Rev. Clement Markham to Clerk, Outlook House, Littleton, New Hampshire:

[*Telegram.*]

BREVOORT HOUSE, NEW YORK, *September 11th.*

Is Mrs. Markham still at Outlook House? Answer prepaid.

XX.

Clerk, Outlook House, to the Rev. Clement Markham, New York:

[*Telegram.*]

LITTLETON, NEW HAMPSHIRE, *September 11th.*

Mrs. Markham left on morning train yesterday for New York.

XXI.

The Rev. Clement Markham to Mr. John Amesbury, Minneapolis:

[*Telegram.*]

BREVOORT HOUSE, NEW YORK, *September 11th.*

Has Mrs. Markham returned to Minneapolis? Please answer immediately.

XXII.

Mr. John Amesbury to the Rev. Clement Markham,
New York:

[*Telegram.*]

MINNEAPOLIS, *September 11th.*

Mrs. Markham has not returned. Glad you are
back safe.

XXIII.

The Rev. Clement Markham to Mr. Ronald Markham, Menger House, San Antonio, Texas:

[*Telegram.*]

BREVOORT HOUSE, NEW YORK, *September 11th.*
[Delivered September 12th.]

Did Margaret communicate with you in regard to
her intended movements ?   I cannot find her and
am much perturbed.   Answer at once.

XXIV.

Mrs. Clement Markham to Mr. Hubert Van Cortlandt, No. — Broadway, New York:

No. 68 CLINTON PLACE, *September 11th.*

DEAR MR. VAN CORTLANDT,—I was so sorry that,
after all, we did miss each other in the crowd last
night.   But I got along very well, thanks to your
forethought in telling me just what to do, though I
must confess that I had five very dreadful minutes

while I was looking for the card on which I had written Mrs. Warden's address. And where do you suppose I found it at last? It was in my pocket-book, just where you told me to put it! Wasn't it absurd? So then we came down here very comfortably, and found the delightful apartment that you had secured for me. As for Mrs. Warden, she is as good as gold. She even had warm milk ready for Teddy, and a delicious cup of tea for me. I never shall be able to thank you enough for all that you have done.

What arrangements have you made about bringing Clement to me? If the dear boy hasn't gone on that slow ship to Boston, and has come, as you think he has, on the *City of Paris*, he ought to arrive to-day. I should love to go down to the dock and be the very first to welcome him. But in such a crowd as there will be I ought not to venture, ought I? Please let me know by bearer just what you have done about our meeting, and when I am to expect my dear boy.

XXV.

Mr. Robert Warrington to Mrs. Clement Markham, No. 68 Clinton Place, New York:

LAW OFFICES OF

VAN CORTLANDT, HOWARD, WARRINGTON & EDGECOMBE, EQUITABLE BUILDING, No. 120 BROADWAY.

NEW YORK, *September 11th.*

Miss (or Mrs.) Margaret Markham:

DEAR MADAM,—Replying, in the absence of Mr.

Van Cortlandt, to yours of even date, I would say that Mr. Van Cortlandt was called out of town suddenly yesterday by the dangerous illness of his wife. I have no knowledge of the matter concerning which you inquire, and regret, therefore, my inability to supply the information which you ask. I may say, however, that the *City of Paris*, as I have ascertained by telephone, arrived at her dock about half an hour ago. Should you desire to telegraph Mr. Van Cortlandt, his address is the Bear and Fox Inn, Tannersville, Greene County, New York.

XXVI.

Mrs. Clement Markham to Mr. Hubert Van Cortlandt, Bear and Fox Inn, Tannersville, Greene County, New York :

[*Telegram.*]

68 CLINTON PLACE, NEW YORK, *September 11th.*
[Delivered September 12th.]

What arrangements did you make for letting Clement know where to find me ? If he came on the *City of Paris* he is here in New York now. I am anxious. So sorry about Mrs. Van Cortlandt.

XXVII.

Mr. Ronald Markham to the Rev. Clement Markham, New York :

[*Telegram.*]

SAN ANTONIO, TEXAS, *September 12th.*

Do not know Margaret's plans. Think she arranged matters with Van Cortlandt. See him.

XXVIII.

Mr. Hubert Van Cortlandt to Mrs. Clement Markham, New York :

[*Telegram.*]

TANNERSVILLE, *September 12th.*

Made no arrangements. Expected to meet Clement at dock. Sorry if I have occasioned you annoyance. You know cause of neglect. Mrs. Van Cortlandt now out of danger.

XXIX.

The Rev. Clement Markham to Mr. Ronald Markham, San Antonio, Texas :

[*Telegram.*]

BREVOORT HOUSE, NEW YORK, *September 12th.*

Van Cortlandt in Catskills with sick wife. Saw his partner, Edgecombe, who can tell me nothing.

I have ascertained that Margaret left Littleton day before yesterday for this city. With her departure from Littleton all trace of her is lost. She has not returned to Minneapolis. I am wellnigh crazed with grief and anxiety. Advise me at once what is best to be done. Shall I advertise? Will it be well to employ the police? For Heaven's sake, answer promptly and fully!

XXX.

Mrs. Clement Markham to Mrs. Winthrop Tremont, Boston :

[*Telegram.*]

68 CLINTON PLACE, NEW YORK, *September 12th.*

City of Paris arrived. Mrs. Warden been to dock and got passenger list. Clement's name in it, so he certainly made mistake in his cable despatch. I state facts fully and clearly, so that you may understand why Mr. Van Cortlandt was called suddenly to see sick wife in Catskills, and so, while Clement must be here in New York, perhaps close by me, am unable to find him, and he, of course, does not in the least know where to find me. There are hundreds of hotels here in New York, and he may be at all of them. I don't know what to do, and am almost frantic with anxiety. Telegraph me at once, dear Aunt Lucy, and make telegram perfectly clear, like mine, and long and full and explicit. This is no time to think about what telegraphing costs. Perhaps Clement has gone on to you, or the other ship may have got

in sooner.   If he is with you, implore him to return
to me at once.   Would it be well for me to employ
the police?   That was my first thought, but I was
afraid that I might make his disappearance get into
the newspapers and be a scandal, and that would not
do for a clergyman.   And he has not really disappeared ; it is only that we neither of us know where
we each are.   My head is one horrible buzz.   Shall
I advertise ?   Had I better offer a reward ?   Give
me your best advice, dear Aunt Lucy, and please
answer immediately.

XXXI.

Mr. Ronald Markham to Mrs. Winthrop Tremont,
    Boston :

[Telegram.]

SAN ANTONIO, TEXAS, *September 12th.*
[Delivered 13th.]

Clement is at Brevoort House, New York.   By
characteristic blunder has missed Margaret.   If you
know her address, please telegraph him.

XXXII.

Mrs. Winthrop Tremont to Mr. Ronald Markham.
New York (forwarded to San Antonio, Texas) :

[Telegram.]

BOSTON, *September 12th.*,
[Delivered 13th.]

Margaret is at No. 68 Clinton Place, in great
10

distress because Clement˙ does not come to her. What foolishness has overtaken these innocents now ? Please set them right.

XXXIII.

Mrs. Winthrop Tremont to Mrs. Clement Markham, No. 68 Clinton Place, New York:

[*Telegram.*]

BOSTON, *September 13th.*

Clement is at the Brevoort House, quite close by you.

XXXIV.

Mr. Ronald Markham to the Rev. Clement Markham, Brevoort House, New York:

[*Telegram.*]

SAN ANTONIO, TEXAS, *September 13th.*

You will find Margaret at No. 68 Clinton Place, directly across the street from your hotel.

XXXV.

Mrs. Clement Markham to Mrs. Winthrop Tremont, Boston:

ST. JUDE'S RECTORY, MINNEAPOLIS, *September 23d.*

DEAR AUNT LUCY,—We left New York early last Monday, and by Tuesday night we were once more safe and together here in our own dear home. We had no misadventures on our journey, except that we nearly missed our connection at Syracuse (where we left the parlor-car for the sleeper) by getting on the wrong train. Fortunately dear Clement found out his mistake just in time.

I had not the energy to do more than telegraph you from New York that all our troubles were ended. I was too much upset by the agony that I had been through to write. It was a very dreadful two days, dear Aunt Lucy; the most dreadful—especially that second day and the last night—that I have ever known. And dear Clement suffered even more than I did, for I knew at least that he was alive, and he knew absolutely nothing about me at all. It all seems now like a horrible dream, and when I shut my eyes and think about it, I turn giddy and feel sick and faint. You cannot possibly imagine, dear Aunt Lucy, how utterly, utterly dreadful it all was!

If it had not been so very dreadful, it would have been a little absurd, I think ; for, you know, all the while that we were in such terrible distress about being unable to find each other, we actually could have opened our windows and talked to each other just across the street! As I found out, when at last dear Clement came to me, his room in the Brevoort House was directly opposite my apartment at No. 68 Clinton Place. Was it not strange? And what was still stranger, dear Aunt Lucy, was that the very morning that our agony ended I happened to look across the street, and there, hanging beside an open window of the hotel, I saw a lovely chasuble that I knew must belong to some clergyman, and it made me think of the chasuble that Clement had written he had bought in London — and it really was that very chasuble, you know, for Clement had hung it there to get the creases out of it—and seeing it set me into a perfect agony of grief, for I thought that I never was to see my dear husband again, and that my children were fatherless, and that I was a widow, and that there was nothing left for me in the world but the blackest despair. And it was while I was crying my very heart out that there was a knock at the door, and then, in a single instant, all my sorrow was ended as I found myself once more in dear Clement's arms.

Yesterday dear Clement preached a beautiful sermon about man's liability to error, and the mysterious ways through which human error providentially is set right. It was a very impressive sermon. In the service he wore his new chasuble. It is exceedingly becoming. Everybody was very much moved by the sermon; and I was moved, of course, most of all. I could not help crying. Dear Clement's voice trembled once or twice, and I saw that there were tears in his eyes. The gloves are perfect, and the stockings really are too good to be true. They are open-work over the ankles, and three of the six pairs are ribbed. I wish that I could tell you what a queer time dear Clement had when he was buying them. He bought them in a French shop in Paris, you know; and when he asked for stockings with narrow ankles, the young woman who was waiting on him— But it will be better to wait until I can tell it to you. It was very funny. And the very best of all, dear Aunt Lucy, is that the surprise that Clement would not write to me about *is* the silk for a new black silk dress! It is a lovely quality. I do wish that you could have heard Clement's beautiful sermon yesterday, and that you could have seen how handsome he looked in his new chasuble. The weather to-day is very warm. The children are wonderfully well.

FOR THE HONOR OF FRANCE.

"Pardon! Madame does not know that this is a smoking-carriage?"

"But yes. Monsieur is very good. It is that my husband would smoke. He is an old soldier. He smokes all the time. *Ciel!* They are like chimneys, these old soldiers. This man of mine regrets that he cannot smoke when he is asleep!"

While Madame delivered this address she continued also to mount the steps, and as she finished it she seated herself in the corner of the carriage opposite to me. She was short and round and sixty years old, and smiling like the sun on a fine day. Her dress was the charming dress of Arles, but over her kerchief she wore a silk mantle that glittered with an embroidery of jet beads. This mantle was precious to her. Her first act upon seating herself was to take it off, fold it carefully in a large handkerchief, and lay it safely in the netting above her head. She replaced it with a red knitted shawl, partly as a shield against the dust, and partly as a protection against the fresh wind that was blowing briskly down the valley of the Rhône.

In a moment her husband followed her, bowing to me as he entered the carriage. Seating himself beside her, and giving her plump hand a little affec-

tionate pat, he said : "It is all right, little one. Marie will receive her jelly in good condition. I myself saw that the basket was placed right side up in
the carriage. The jelly will not spill." Then, turning to me, he added : "My wife makes a wonderful
jelly of apricots, Monsieur. We are taking some of
it to our married daughter, who lives in Avignon."

He was a well set-up old boy, with a face most
pleasantly frank, close - cut gray hair, short gray
whiskers, and a bristling white mustache. Across
his forehead, cutting through his right eyebrow, was
a desperate scar, that I at once associated in my own
mind with the red ribbon of the Legion that he
wore in the button-hole of his black frock-coat. He
looked the officer in retreat, and the very gentleness
and sweetness of his manner made me sure that he
had done some gallant fighting in his time.

As the train pulled out from the station—it was
at Tarascon that they had joined me—he drew forth
from his pocket a black little wooden pipe and a tobacco-bag. This was my opportunity. I also drew
forth a pipe and a tobacco-bag. Would Monsieur
accept some of my tobacco? I asked. I had brought
it, I added, from America ; it was tobacco of the
Havana.

"Monsieur then is an American. That is interesting. And his tobacco is from the Havana, that is
more interesting still. My cousin's son has been for
many years in America. His name is Marius Gui-
raud ; he lives in San Francisco ; possibly Monsieur
and he have met ?"

Monsieur regretted that he had not had this pleasure, and explained that his home was in New York—three times as far from San Francisco as Marseilles was from Paris.

"Name of a name! Is it possible? How vast this America must be! And they tell me—" Here he struck a wax match and paused to light his pipe. He drew a dozen whiffs in silence, while on his face was the thoughtful look of one whose taste in tobacco was critical and whose love for it was strong.

"Thunder of guns, but it is good!" he exclaimed, as he took the pipe from his mouth and passed it lightly back and forth beneath his nose. "Had we smoked tobacco like this in the Crimea we should have whipped those rascal Russians in a single week. Ah, that we often were without tobacco was the hardest part of all. I have smoked coffee grounds and hay, Monsieur, and have been thankful to get them—I myself, who well know what is good and what is not good in a pipe! This tobacco—it is divine!"

"Monsieur served in the Crimea?"

"This is the proof of it," he said, a little grimly, touching the scar on his forehead.

"And this," his wife added, touching the bit of red ribbon in his button-hole. "He was the bravest man in all that war, Monsieur, this old husband of mine. His cross was given him by—"

"Tchut, little one! What does Monsieur care how I got my cross? It was not much that I did. Any man would have done the same."

"But the others did *not* do the same. They ran away and left thee to do it alone. Did not his Majesty tell thee—"

"Ah, Monsieur hears what a *babillarde* it is. If she were given her own way she would swear that I commanded the allied armies, and that I blew up the Redan and stormed the Malakoff and captured Sebastopol all alone !"

"Tell Monsieur what thou didst do," said the little woman, warmly. "Tell him truly precisely what thou didst do, and then let him judge for himself if what I have said be one bit less than thy due."

"And so bring Monsieur to know that I am a babbling old woman like thyself ?" He pinched her gently, and then settled himself back against the cushion as though with the intention of giving himself wholly to the enjoyment of his pipe: yet was there a look in his eyes that showed how strong was the desire within him—the desire that is natural to every brave and simple-minded old soldier—to tell the story of his honorable scars. Even had I felt no desire to hear this story, not to have pressed him to tell it would have been cruel. But little pressing was required.

"Since Monsieur is good enough to desire to hear what little there is to tell," he said, "and to show him how foolish is this old woman of mine, I will tell him the whole affair. It is a stupid nothing ; but Monsieur may be amused by the trick that was put upon me by those great generals—yes, that certainly was droll.

"Our regiment, Monsieur, was the Twenty-seventh
of the Line. It was drawn almost wholly from the
towns and villages in these parts: Arles and Tarascon and Saint-Remy and Salon and Maillane and
Château Renard—there is the old château, over on
the hill yonder, beside the Durance—and Barben-
tane, that we shall see presently around the corner
of the hill. We all were *Provençaux* together, and
the men of the other regiments of our division gave
us the name of the Provence cats; though why they
gave us that foolish name I am sure they never knew
any more than we did ourselves. It was not because
we were cowards, that I will swear: our regiment
did some very pretty fighting in its time, as any one
may know by reading the gazettes which were published in those days.

"Our division held Mont Sapoune—the French
right, you know—facing the Little Redan across the
Carenage Ravine. It was early in the siege, and we
had only drawn our first parallel: close against the
Selinghinsk and Vallyrie redoubts, and partly cov-
ering the ground where we dug our rifle-pits later
on. But we were going ahead with our work fast,
and already we had thrown up the little redoubts
known as No. 11 and No. 15, which covered the ad-
vancing earthwork leading to where our second parallel was to begin. Redoubt No. 11 was a good hundred yards, and Redoubt No. 15 was more than three
times that distance outside of our lines; and everybody knew that these two advanced posts would be
in great danger until our second parallel was well

under way. So very possible was it that they might be surprised, and the guns turned on our own lines in support of a general attack, that in each of them spikes and hammers were kept in readiness against the need for spiking the guns before they fell into the enemy's hands. Our regiment lay just behind these redoubts, in the rear of the artillerymen who manned our trenches; and as the gunners had plenty to do all day long, and through the night too sometimes, the work of keeping up the night pickets fell to our share.

"It was while things were this way that I was on picket early one morning on our extreme left, close over the edge of the Carenage Ravine. I had come on with the midnight relief, and by five o'clock in the morning, when day was just breaking, my teeth were chattering and I was stiff with cold. Name of a name, but it was cold those winter mornings! We have nothing like it, even when the worst mistral is blowing, in our winters here in Provence. Down in the ravine there was a thick mist, into which I could not see at all; but every now and then a whiff of wind would come in from the seaward and thin it a little, and then I would give a good look below me, for it was along the ravine that any party sent out to surprise us almost certainly would come.

"It was while the light still was faint that I thought I heard, coming up through the mist, a little rattling sound, such as might be made by a man stumbling and dropping his musket among the bro-

ken rocks. Just then the mist was too thick for me
to see twenty feet below me. I was sure that something bad was going on down there, but I did not
want to make a fool of myself by giving a false
alarm. All that I could do was to cock my musket
and to hold it pointed towards where the sound
seemed to come from, all ready, should there be
need for it, to give the alarm and get in a shot at
the enemy at the same time. Truly, Monsieur, it
seemed to me that I stood that way, while my heart
went pounding against my ribs, for a whole year!
I was no longer cold : the blood was racing through
my veins, and I was everywhere in a glow. Suddenly there came a puff of wind, and as the mist
thinned for a moment I saw that the whole ravine
was full of Russians. Their advance already was
half-way up the bank nearest to our works. In less
than ten minutes the whole of them would be dashing into our outlying redoubts. As I pulled the trig-
ger of my musket I tried to shout, but my throat
was as dry as a furnace and I could only gasp. And
—will you believe it?—my musket missed fire!
Name of a name, what a state I was in! There was
the enemy coming on under cover of the mist ; and
there was I, the only man who could save our army,
standing dumb like a useless fool!

"What I must do came to me like a flash. If I
ran back inside of our lines to give the alarm, the
chances were a thousand to one that the enemy
would have the outlying redoubt, very likely would
have them both, and would turn the guns before

help could come. But I knew, at least I hoped, that there was time for me to get to the more exposed redoubt ahead of them and give the word to spike the guns. It was all in an instant, I say, that I found this thought in my mind, and my musket and cartridge-box thrown I don't know where, and myself dashing off through the mist across the broken ground like a deer.

"As I rushed into the redoubt our men thought that I was the Russians; and when they knew me by my uniform for a Frenchman, and heard me crying in a hoarse whisper, 'Spike the guns!' they thought that I was mad. But the lieutenant in command of the battery had at least a little sense, even if he did not have much courage, and he looked towards where I pointed—and then he saw the shakos, as the mist lifted again, not a hundred feet away.

"'Save yourselves, I will make the guns safe,' he cried to his men—he was not all a coward, poor fellow —and as they ran for it he picked up the spikes and the hammer. Tap! tap! tap! one gun was spiked. Tap! tap! tap! another. Then we heard the Russians beginning to scramble up outside.

"He swore a great oath as he dropped the hammer. 'It can't be done. Run, cat!' he cried—and away he started after his men. The name that I called him as he ran away, Monsieur, was a very foul name; God forgive me for what I said! But I was determined that it *should* be done. In a second I had picked up the nails and the hammer, and—tap! tap! tap!—the third gun was safe. 'Run, cat!' I heard the lieutenant call again. But—tap!—I had the nail started in the last gun, and then, right above me, was a Russian major and with him a dozen of his men. Tap! and I had the nail half-way home as the major jumped down beside me, with his sword raised. I knew that I could parry his blow with the hammer and then, possibly, get away; but I wanted to make sure that that gun could not be turned. And so—it was quick thinking that I did just then, Monsieur—tap! and the gun was no better than old iron! At that same instant it seemed to me that the whole world burst into a tremendous roar and ten thousand blazing stars—but it only was the sword of that confounded Russian major banging against my skull!"

The little woman was almost sobbing. She took her husband's hand in both of hers.

"But you see that I was *not* killed, little one," he said; and he raised her hands to his lips and kissed them.

"It was not until the next day, Monsieur," he went on, "that I knew anything. Then I was in the hospital.

"'How did it go?' I asked of the hospital-steward.

"'Shut up,' said the steward.

"This made me angry. 'How did it go, *polisson?*' I cried. 'Tell me, or I'll crush your bones.'

"Then the man was more civil. 'The Russians were driven back,' he said, 'and a lot of them were captured. You owe it to the same Russian major

11

who almost killed you that your life was saved. As soon as he was brought into camp he sent a message to the general begging that you might be looked after quickly. If there was any life left in you, it was worth saving, he said, for you were a brave man— and he told how you had spiked those last two guns. *Parbleu*, but for that message you would have died! When they brought you in here you were nearly gone!'

"'And the lieutenant who ran away?' I asked.

"'Oh, he was killed—as he deserved. Now you know all about it. Hold your tongue.'

"I felt so foolishly weak, and there was such a pain in my head as I began to remember it all once more, that I could not ask any more questions. Presently my head began to buzz and the pain in it to get worse, and then for a week I had a fever that came near to taking me off. But I pulled through" —he squeezed his wife's hand, that again had been laid in his—"and in three weeks I was back with the regiment again. It was all due to my having such a wonderfully thick skull, the doctors said, that the major's sword had not broken it past all mending. When I came into camp the boys all cheered me, and I was as proud as a cock. And then, the first thing I knew, up came a corporal and a file of men and arrested me.

"'What am I arrested for?' I asked.

"'For being absent without leave from your regiment during battle,' said the corporal, and marched me off to the guard-house. Then I was not proud at all. But I was very angry. That I should be arrested in this fashion did not seem to me fair.

"In half an hour back came the corporal and his file of men. This time they took me to headquarters. In we went; and the corporal stood beside me, and his men behind me in a row. It seemed as though half the officers of our army were there: my colonel, the general of our brigade, the general of our division, half a dozen other generals, three or four English officers in their smart red coats; presently there was a stir—and in came the Emperor! What the deuce it all meant I could not tell at all!

"'Private Labonne,' said my colonel, he spoke in a very harsh tone, yet it seemed to me that there was an odd sort of twinkle in his eye—'you deserted your post, and you were absent without leave when your regiment went into action.'

"'Yes, but—'

"'Not a word of excuse, Private Labonne. You know the penalty.' I did know the penalty, of course; it was to be taken out and shot. I began to think that this was worse than the Russians!

"'When shall I order the court-martial, your Majesty?' asked my colonel.

"'I will be the court-martial,' said the Emperor. 'This is a serious matter; this is a matter to be dealt with in a hurry. The case is proved. There is no need for a trial. I order Private Labonne to be shot right away.'

"I shivered all down my back. It *was* worse than the Russians; very much worse.

" 'Take him away,' said my colonel.

" The corporal put his hand on my shoulder and the guard closed in.   'March !' said the corporal.

" 'Stop !' said the Emperor.   'Private Labonne, before you are taken away and shot, tell me what you were doing in that battery.'

" 'Nothing, your Majesty.'

" 'Nothing ?   I thought that I heard something about guns being spiked.   Did not you spike a gun, Private Labonne ?'

" 'Yes, your Majesty.'

" 'Did not you spike two guns—and both of them after the gunners and the officer in command of the battery had run away ?'

" 'Yes, your Majesty.'

" 'And why did you not run away, too, Private Labonne ?'

" 'Because I wanted to spike the guns, your Majesty.'

" 'You did not think, then, that it was your duty as one of my soldiers to save your life by running with the others ?'

" This question puzzled me, for I certainly never had thought of the matter in that way at all.   It occurred to me that perhaps I really had not done my duty.   But what the Emperor said, for all that he was the Emperor, did not seem reasonable, and I made bold to answer him : 'If I had taken care of my own life, your Majesty, a great many of your soldiers would have died to pay for it.   It would have been a bad day's work if those two guns had not been spiked, for the Russians certainly would have turned them on our lines.'

"The Emperor turned to my colonel. 'There is something in what Private Labonne says, eh, colonel? I suppose there really would have been the very devil to pay had the enemy turned those guns?'

"'I suppose there would,' said my colonel, a little grimly.

"'Then the case is not quite so black against Private Labonne as it at first appeared?'

"'Not quite so black,' said my colonel.

"'Perhaps we need not have him shot, after all?'

"'Perhaps not—not this time, at least.'

"'We might even compliment him a little upon his bravery. For it was rather brave—eh, colonel? —to stay in that battery and spike those guns, while a hundred Russians were tumbling in upon him, and his own comrades had run off and left him to do his duty and to die for it there alone.'

"My colonel's voice broke a little as he answered, 'It was very brave, your Majesty.'

"'Eh, well, Private Labonne,' said the Emperor, turning again to me, 'we won't shoot you. Your colonel is right about your bravery; and to shoot a brave man, except in battle, is a mistake. The Russian officer who came so near to killing you was a major, I am told; well, you may happen to meet him again, and if you do it is only fair that your rank should equal his. Here is your commission, Major Labonne; and here is a little thing '—it was his own cross of the Legion that the Emperor gave me—

'that I want you to wear in remembrance of that day when you did as brave a piece of work as ever was done by a French soldier for the honor of France !'

"And so you see, Monsieur, it was only a comedy about my being shot, after all. Here is Avignon. You must wait for me a moment, little one, while I get the basket of jelly for Marie."

A ROMANCE OF TOMPKINS SQUARE.

WHETHER the honey shall be brought to the boiling-point slowly or rapidly; whether it shall boil a long time or a short time; when and in what quantities the flour shall be added; how long the kneading shall last; in what size of earthen pot the dough shall be stored, and what manner of cover upon these pots best preserves the dough against the assaults of damp and mould; whether the pots shall be half-buried in the cool earth of the cellar or ranged on shelves to be freely exposed to the cool cellar air—all these several matters are enshrouded in a mystery that is penetrated only by the elect few of Nürnberg bakers by whom perfect lebkuchen is made. And the same is true of the Brunswick bakers, who call this rare compound honigkuchen, and of the makers of pferfferkuchen, as it is called by the bakers of Saxony.

Nor does the mystery end here. This first stage in the making of lebkuchen is but means to an end, and for the compassing of that end—the blending and the baking of the finished and perfect honey-cake—each master-baker has his own especial recipe, that has come down to him from some ancestral baker of rare parts, or that by his own inborn genius has been directly inspired. And so, whether the toothsome result be Nürnberger lebkuchen, or Brunsscheiger peppernotte, or Basler leckerly, the making of it is a mystery from first to last.

It was because of this mystery that the life of Gottlieb Brekel had been imbittered for nearly twenty years—ever since, in fact, his first essay in the compounding of Nürnberger lebkuchen had been made. He was but a young baker then: now he was an old one, and notwithstanding the guarded praise of friends and the partial approval of the public (notably of that portion of the public under the age of ten years that attended St. Bridget's Parochial School) he full well knew that his efforts through all these years to make, in New York, lebkuchen such as he himself had eaten when he was a boy, at home in Nürnberg, had been neither more nor less than a long series of failures.

In the hopeful days of his apprenticeship all had seemed so easy before him. Let him but have a little shop, and then a little capital wherewith to lay in his supply of honey, and the thing would be done! He had no recipe, it is true; for he was a baker not by heredity, but by selection. Yet from a wise old baker he had gleaned the knowledge of honey-cake making, and he believed strongly that from the pure fount of his own genius he could draw a formula for the making of lebkuchen so excellent that compared with it all other lebkuchen would seem tasteless. But these were the bright dreams of youth, which age had refused to realize.

In course of time the little shop became an accom-

plished fact; a very little shop it was in East Fourth
Street.   Capital came more slowly, and three several
times, when a sum almost sufficient had been saved,
was it diverted from its destined purpose of buying
the honey without which Gottlieb could not make
even a beginning in his triumphal lebkuchen career.

His first accumulation was swept away through
the conquest of Ambition by Love.   In this case
Love was personified in one Minna Schaus—who
was not by any means a typical sturdy German lass,
with laughing looks and stalwart ways, but a dainti-
ly-finished, golden-haired maiden, with soft blue eyes
full of tenderness, and a gentleness of manner that
Gottlieb thought—and with more reason than lovers
sometimes think things of this sort—was very like
the manner of an angel.   And for love of her Gottlieb forgot for a while his high resolves in regard to
lebkuchen making; and on the altar of his affec-
tions—in part to pay for his modest wedding-feast,
in part to pay for the modest outfit for their house-
keeping over the bakery—the money laid aside for
the filling of his honey-pots very willingly was offered up.

A second time were his honey-pots sacrificed, that
the coming into the world of the little Minna might
be made smooth.   This, also, was a willing sacrifice;
though in his heart of hearts Gottlieb felt a twinge
of regret that his first-born was not a son, to whom
the fame and fortune incident to the making of perfect lebkuchen might descend.   But he was a phi-
losopher in his way, and did not suffer himself to be

seriously disconcerted by an accident that by no means was irreparable. As he smoked his long pipe that night, while the bread was baking, he said to himself, cheerily: "It is a girl. Yes, that is easy. Girls sprout everywhere; they are like grass. But a boy, and a boy who is to grow up into such a baker as my boy will be—ah, that is another matter. But patience, Gottlieb; all in good time." Then, when his third pipe was finished—which was his measure of time for the baking—he fetched out the sweet-smelling hot bread from the oven with his long peel, and set forth upon his round of delivery. And he whistled a mellow old Nürnberg air as he pushed his cart through the streets before him that frosty morning, and in his heart he thanked the good God who had sent him the blessings of a dear wife and a sweet little daughter and a growing trade.

And yet once more were his honey-pots sacrificed, and this time the sacrifice was sad indeed. From the day that the little Minna came into the world his own Minna, as in a little while was but too plain to him, began to make ready to leave it. As the weeks went by, the little strength that at first had come to her was lost again; the faint color faded from her cheeks, and left them so wan that through the fair skin the blue veins showed in most delicate tracery; and as her dear eyes ever grew gentler and more loving, the light slowly went out from them. So within the year the end came. In that great sorrow Gottlieb forgot his ambition, and cared not, when the bills were paid, that his honey-pots still remained

unfilled. For the care of his home and of little Minna
his good sister Hedwig came to him. Very drearily,
for a long while, the work of the bakery went on.

But a strong man, stirred by a strong purpose,
does not relinquish that purpose lightly; and the one
redeeming feature of the life of many sorrows
which in this world we all are condemned to live is
that even the bitterest sorrow is softened by time.
But for this partial relief our race no doubt would
have been extinguished ages ago in a madness
wrought of grief and rage.

Gottlieb's strong purpose was to make the best
lebkuchen that baker ever baked. After a fashion
his sorrow healed, as the flesh heals about a bullet
that has gone too deep to be extracted by the sur-
geon's craft, and while it was with him always, and
not seldom sent through all his being thrills of pain,
he bore it hidden from the world, and went about
his work again. Working comforted him. The
baking of bread is an employment that is at once
soothing and sustaining. As a man kneads the
spongy dough he has good exercise and wholesome
time for thought. While the baking goes on he may
smoke and meditate. The smell of the newly-baked
bread is a pleasant smell, and brings with it pleasant
thoughts of many people well nourished in the eating of it. Moreover, there is no time in the whole
twenty-four hours when a city is so innocent, so like
the quiet honest country-side, as that time in the
crisp morning when a baker goes his rounds.

As Gottlieb found himself refreshed and strength-

ened by these manifold good influences of his gentle
trade, his burden of sorrow was softened to him and
made easier to bear. Comforting thoughts of the little Minna—growing to be a fine little lass now—stole
in upon him, and within him the hope arose that she
would grow to be like the dear mother whom she
never had known. So the little fine roots of a new
love struck down into his sad heart; and presently
the sweet plant of love began to grow for him
again, casting its delicate tendrils strongly about the
child, who truly was a part of the being about which
his earlier and stronger love had clung. Yet the
love that thus was re-established in Gottlieb's breast
was far from filling it, and so for ambition there was
ample room.

Somewhat to his surprise, one night, as he sat beside the oven smoking his second pipe, he found
himself thinking once more about his project for
making such lebkuchen as never yet had been known
outside of Nürnberg—lebkuchen that would make
him at once the admiration and the despair of every
German baker in New York. Nor was there, as he
perceived as he turned the matter over in his mind,
any reason now why he should not set about making this project a reality ; for he had money enough,
and more than enough, in store to buy the honey
that he had so long desired. His eyes sparkled; he
forgot to smoke ; and when he turned again, half un-
consciously, to his pipe, it had gone out. This roused
him. The brightness faded from his eyes; he drew
a long sigh. Then he lighted his pipe again, and

"One night, as he sat beside the oven smoking his second pipe, he found himself thinking."

until the baking was ended his thoughts no longer
were busied with ambitious schemes for the making
of lebkuchen, but went back with a sad tenderness
to the happy time that had come so quickly tc so
cruel an end.

But the spark was kindled, and presently the fire
burned.   When he told the good Hedwig that he
had bought the honey at last, that excellent woman
—albeit not much given to display of the tender
emotions—shed tears of joy.   She was a sturdy,
thick-waisted, stout-ankled person, this Aunt Hedwig, with a cheery red face, and prodigiously fine
white teeth, and very bright black eyes; and her
taste in dress was such that when of a Sunday she
went to the Church of the Redemptorist Fathers, in
Third Street, she was more brilliant than ever King
Solomon was in all his glory, in her startling array
of vivid reds and greens and blues.   But beneath
her violent exterior of energetic color she had a
warm and faithful heart, as little Minna knew already, and as her brother Gottlieb had known for
many a long good year.   Therefore was Gottlieb
now gladdened by her hearty show of sympathy;
and he returned with a good will the sounding
smack that she gave him with her red lips, and the
strong hug that she gave him w'th her stout arms.

It was at sight of this pleasing manifestation of
affection that Herr Sohnstein, the notary—who was
present in the little room back of the shop where it
occurred—at once declared that he meant to buy
some honey too.   And Aunt Hedwig, smiling so

generously as to show every one of her fine white
teeth, promptly told him that he had better be off
and buy it, because perhaps he could buy at the
same place some hugs and kisses too : at which
sally and quick repartee they all laughed. Herr
Sohnstein long had been the declared lover of Aunt
Hedwig's, and long had been held at arm's-length
(quite literally occasionally) by that vigorous person; who believed, because of her good heart, that
her present duty was not to consult her own happiness by becoming Frau Sohnstein, but to remain the
Fräulein Brekel, and care for her lonely brother and
her brother's child.

Being thus encouraged, Gottlieb bought the honey
forthwith ; and with Aunt Hedwig's zealous assistance set about boiling it and straining it and kneading it into a sticky dough, all in accordance with the
wise old baker's directions which he so long had treas-
ured in his mind. And when the dough was packed
in earthen pots, over which bladders were tied, all
the pots were set away in the coolest part of the
cellar, as far from the great oven as possible, that
the precious honey-cake might undergo that subtle
change which only comes with time.

For at least a year must pass before the honey-
cake really can be said to be good at all ; and the
longer that it remains in the pots, even until five-
and-twenty years, the better does it become. Therefore it is that all makers of lebkuchen who aspire to
become famous professors of the craft add each
year to their stock of honey-cake, yet draw always

"When the dough was packed in earthen pots, over which bladders were tied, the pots were set away in the coolest part of the cellar."

from the oldest pots a time-soaked dough that ever
grows more precious in its sweet excellence of age.
Thus large sums—more hundreds of dollars than a
young baker, just starting upon his farinaceous career, would dare to dream of—may be invested;
and the old rich bakers who can dower their daughters with many honey-pots know that in the matter
of sons-in-law they have but to pick and choose.

It was about Christmas-time—which is the proper
time for this office—that Gottlieb made his first
honey-cake; and it was a little before the Christmas following that his first lebkuchen was baked.
For a whole week before this portentous event occurred he was in a nervous tremor; by day he
scarcely slept; as he sat beside the oven at night
his pipe so frequently went out that twice, having
thus lost track of time, his baking of bread came
near to being toast. And when at last the fateful
night arrived that saw his first batch of lebkuchen
in the oven, he actually forgot to smoke at all!

Gottlieb had but a sorry Christmas that year.
The best that even Aunt Hedwig could say of his
lebkuchen was that it was not bad. Herr Sohnstein,
to be sure, brazenly declared that it was delicious;
but Gottlieb remembered that Herr Sohnstein, who
conducted a flourishing practice in the criminal
courts, was trained in the art of romantic devia-
tions from the truth whenever it was necessary to
put a good face on a bad cause; and he observed
sadly that the notary's teeth were at variance with
his tongue, for the piece of lebkuchen that Herr

12

Sohnstein ate was infinitessimally small.   As for
the regular German customers of the bakery, they
simply bit one single bite and then refused to buy.
Indeed, but for the children from St. Bridget's
School — who, being for the most part boys, and
Irish boys at that, presumably could eat anything—
it is not impossible that that first baking of lebkuchen might have remained uneaten even until this
present day.   And it was due mainly to the stout
stomachs of successive generations of these enter-
prising boys that the series of experiments which
Gottlieb then began in the making of lebkuchen
was brought, in the course of years, to something
like a satisfactory conclusion.   But even at its best,
never was this lebkuchen at all like that of which in
his hopeful youth he had dreamed.

Herr Sohnstein, to be sure, spoke highly of it, and
even managed to eat of it quite considerable quantities.   Gottlieb did not imagine that Herr Sohnstein
could have in this matter any ulterior motives; but
Aunt Hedwig much more than half suspected that
in order to please her by pleasing her brother he was
making a sacrifice of his stomach to his heart.   If
this theory had any foundation in fact, it is certain
that Herr Sohnstein did not appreciably profit by
his gallant risk of indigestion; for while Aunt Hedwig by no means seemed disposed to shatter all his
hopes by a sharp refusal, she gave no indication
whatever of any intention to permit her ripe red
lips to utter the longed-for word of assent.   Aunt
Hedwig, unquestionably, was needlessly cruel in her

treatment of Herr Sohnstein, and he frequently told
her so. Sometimes he would ask her, with a fine
irony, if she meant to keep him waiting for his
answer until her brother had made lebkuchen as
good as the lebkuchen of Nürnberg? To which
invariably she would reply that, in the first place,
she did not know of any question that he ever had
asked her that required an answer; and, in the
second place, that she did mean to keep him waiting just precisely that long. And then she would
add, with a delicate drollery that was all her own,
that whenever he got tired of waiting he might hire
a whole horse-car all to himself and ride right
away. Ah, this Aunt Hedwig had a funny way with
her!

And so the years slipped by; and little Minna, who
laughed at the passing years as merrily as Aunt Hedwig laughed at Herr Sohnstein, grew up into a blithe,
trig, round maiden, and ceased to be little Minna at
all. She was her mother over again, Gottlieb said;
but this was not by any means true. She did have
her mother's goodness and sweetness, but her sturdy
body bespoke her father's stronger strain. Aunt
Hedwig, of this same strain, undisguisedly was
stocky. Minna was only comfortably stout, with
good broad shoulders, and an honest round waist
that anybody with half an eye for waists could see
would be a satisfactory armful. And she had also
Aunt Hedwig's constant cheeriness. All day long
her laugh sounded happily through the house, or her
voice went blithely in happy talk, or, failing anybody

to talk to, trilled out some scrap of a sweet old German song. The two apprentices and the young man who drove the bread-wagon of course were wildly and desperately in love with her—a tender passion that they dared not disclose to its object, but that they frequently and boastingly aired to each other. Naturally these interchanges of confidence were apt to be somewhat tempestuous. As the result of one of them, when the elder apprentice had declared that Minna's beautiful brown hair was finer than any wig in the window of the hair-dresser on the west side of the square, and that she had given him a lock of it; and when the young man who drove the bread-wagon (he was a profane young man) had declared that it was a verdammter sight finer than any wig, and that she hadn't—the elder apprentice got a dreadful black eye, and the younger apprentice was almost smothered in the dough-trough, and the young man who drove the bread-wagon had his head broken with the peel that was broken over it. Aunt Hedwig did not need to be told, nor did Minna, the little jade, the cause of this direful combat; and both of these amiable women thought Gottlieb very hard-hearted because he charged the broken peel—it was a new one—and the considerable amount of dough that was wasted by sticking to the younger apprentice's person, against the wages of the three combatants.

This reference to the apprentices and to the wagon shows that Gottlieb's bakery no longer was a small bakery, but a large one. In the making of

"The young apprentice was almost smothered in the dough-trough and the young man who drove the bread-wagon had his head broken with the peel."

lebkuchen, it is true, he had not prospered ; but in all other ways he had prospered amazingly. From Avenue A over to the East River, and from far below Tompkins Square clear away to the upper regions of Lexington Avenue, the young man who drove the bread-wagon rattled along every morning as hard as ever he could go, and he vowed and declared, this young man did, that nothing but his love for Minna kept him in a place where all the year round he was compelled in every single day to do the work of two. Meanwhile the little shop on East Fourth Street had been abandoned for a bigger shop, and this, in turn, for one still bigger—quite a palace of a shop, with plate-glass windows—on Avenue B. It was here, beginning in a modest way with a couple of tables whereat chance-hungry people might sit while they ate zwieback or a thick slice of hearty pumpernickel and drank a glass of milk, that a restaurant was established as a tender to the bakery. It did not set out to be a large restaurant, and, in fact, never became one. In the back part of the shop were a dozen tables, covered with oil-cloth and decorated with red napkins, and at these tables, under the especial direction of Aunt Hedwig, who was a culinary genius, was served a limited, but from a German stand-point most toothsome, bill of fare. There was Hasenpfeffer mit Spätzle, and Sauerbraten mit Kartoffelklösse, and Rindfleisch mit Meerrettig, and Bratwurst mit Rothkraut ; and Aunt Hedwig made delicious coffee, and the bakery of course provided all manner of sweet cakes. In the sum-

mer - time they did a famous business in ice-
cream.

On the plate-glass windows beneath the sweeping
curve of white letters in which the name of the owner of the bakery was set forth was added in smaller
letters the words " Café Nürnberger." Gottlieb and
Aunt Hedwig and the man who made the sign (this
last, however, for the venal reason that more letters
would be required) had stood out stoutly for the
honest German "Kaffehaus;" but Minna, whose
tastes were refined, had insisted upon the use of
the French word : there was more style about it,
she said. And this was a case in which style was
wedded to substantial excellence. What with the
good things which Gottlieb baked and the good
things which Aunt Hedwig cooked, the Café Nürnberger presently acquired a somewhat enviable reputation. It became even a resort of the aristocracy,
in this case represented by the dwellers in the handsome houses on the eastern and northern sides of
Tompkins Square. Of winter evenings, when bright
gas-light and a big glowing stove made the restaurant a very cozy place indeed, large parties of these
aristocrats would drop in on their way home from
the Thalia Theatre, and would stuff themselves with
Hasenpfeffer and Sauerbraten and Kartoffelklösse,
and would swig Aunt Hedwig's strong coffee (out of
cups big enough and thick enough to have served as
shells and been fired from a mortar), until it would
seem as though they must certainly crack their aristocratic skins.

Altogether, Gottlieb was in a flourishing line of business; and but for the deep sorrow that time never wholly could heal, and but for the continued failure of his attempts to make a really excellent leb-kuchen, he would have been a very happy man. By this time he had come to be a baker of ease. The hard part of the work was done by the apprentices, and the morning delivery of bread was attended to by the young man who drove the bread-wagon. In the summer-time he would take Minna and Aunt Hed-wig, always accompanied by her faithful Herr Sohn-stein, upon beer-drinking expeditions to Guttenberg and other fashionable suburban resorts; and through the cozy winter evenings he smoked his long pipe comfortably in the little room at the back of the shop, where Minna and Aunt Hedwig sat with him, and where Herr Sohnstein, also smoking a long pipe, usually sat with him too. Sometimes Minna would sing sweet German songs to them, accompanying herself very creditably upon a cabinet organ—for Minna had received not only the substantial educa-tion that enabled her to keep the bakery accounts, but also had been instructed in the polite accom-plishments of music and the dance. In summer, when expeditions were not on foot, these smoking parties usually were held upon the roof; where Gott-lieb had made a garden and grew roses in pots, and even had raised some rare and delicious cauliflowers.

It was a pleasant place, that roof, of a warm sum-mer evening, especially when the rising full-moon sent a shimmering path of glory across the rippling waters of the East River, and cast over the bad-smelling region of Hunter's Point a glamour of golden haze that made it seem, oil tanks and all, a bit of fairy-land. At such times, as they sat among the rose-bushes and cauliflowers, Herr Sohnstein not infrequently would stop smoking his long pipe while he slyly squeezed Aunt Hedwig's plump hand. And Gottlieb also would stop smoking, as his thoughts wandered away along that glittering path across the waters, and so up to heaven where his Minna was. And then his thoughts would return to earth, to his little Minna—for to him she still was but a child— and he would find his sorrow lessened in thankfulness that, while his greatest treasure was lost to him, this good daughter and so many other good things still were his.

But the lebkuchen dream of Gottlieb's youth remained unrealized ; still unattained was the goal that twenty years before had seemed so near. However, being a stout-hearted baker of the solid Nürnberg strain, he did not at all surrender hope. Each year he added to his stock of honey-cake; and he knew that when fortune favored him at last, as he still believed that fortune would favor him, he would have in store such honey-cake as would enable him to make lebkuchen fit to be eaten by the Kaiser himself !

After the affair of the broken peel there was a coolness between Gottlieb and the elder apprentice, which, increasing, led to a positive coldness, and then to a separation. And then it was that Fate put

a large spoke in all the wheels which ran in the Café
Nürnberg by bringing into Gottlieb's employment
a ruddy young Nürnberger, lately come out of that
ancient city to America, named Hans Kuhn.

It was not chance that led Hans to earn his living
in a bakery when he came to New York. He was a
born baker : a baker by choice, by force of natural
genius, by hereditary right. Back in the dusk of
the Middle Ages, as far as ever the traditions of his
family and the records of the Guild of Bakers of
Nürnberg ran, all the men of his race had been
bakers, and famous ones at that. A cumulative
destiny to bake was upon him, and he loved baking
with all his heart. It was no desire to abandon his
craft that had led him to leave Nürnberg and cross
the ocean; rather was he moved by a noble ambition to build up on a broad and sure foundation the
noble art of baking in the New World. And it had
chanced, moreover, that in the conscription he had
drawn an unlucky number.

When this young man entered the Café Nürnberg
—being drawn thither by its display of the name of
his own native city—and asked for a job, his air was
so frank, his talk about baking so intelligent, that
Gottlieb took kindly to him at once; and Minna,
sitting demurely at her accounts in the little wire
cage over which was a fine tin sign inscribed in
golden letters with the word " Cashier," was mightily
well pleased, in a demure and proper way, at sight
of his ruddy cheeks and bushy shock of light-brown
hair and little yellow mustache and honest blue

eyes. When he told, in answer to Gottlieb's questions, that he was the grandson of the very baker in
Nürnberg whose delicious lebkuchen Gottlieb had
eaten when he was a boy, and that a part of his
bakerly equipment was the lebkuchen recipe that
had come down in his family from the baker genius,
his remote ancestor, who had invented it — well,
when he had told this much about himself, it is not
surprising that Gottlieb fairly jumped for joy, and
engaged him, not as his apprentice, but as his assistant, on the spot.

It was rather dashing to Gottlieb's enthusiasm,
however, that his assistant—thereby manifesting a
shrewd worldly wisdom — declined immediately to
impart his secret. He would make all the lebkuchen
that was required, he said, but for the present he
need not tell how it was made—possibly the Herr
Brekel might not be satisfied with it, after all. But
the Herr Brekel was satisfied with it, and so was all
the neighborhood when the first batch of lebkuchen
was baked and placed on sale. Indeed, as the fame
of this delicious lebkuchen went abroad, the coming
of the new baker was accepted by all Germans with
discriminating palates as one of the most important
events that ever had occurred on the East Side.
The work of the young man who drove the bread-
wagon was so greatly increased that he organized a
strike, uniting in his own person the several func-
tions of strikers, walking delegates, district assem-
bly, and executive committee. And when the strike
collapsed—that is to say, when the young man was

discharged summarily — Gottlieb really did find it
necessary to hire two new young men, and to buy
an extra horse and wagon.   Morally speaking, therefore (although the original young man, who remained out of employment for several weeks, and had a
pretty hard time of it, did not think so), the strike
was a complete success.

As a matter of course no well-set-up, right-think-
ing young fellow of three-and-twenty could go on
baking lebkuchen in the same bakery with Minna
Brekel for any length of time without falling in
love with her.   Nor was it reasonable to suppose
that even Minna, who had treated casual apprentices
and wagon-driving young men with a seemly scorn,
would continue to sit in the seat of the scornful
when siege in form was laid to her heart by a properly ruddy-cheeked and blue-eyed assistant baker,
whose skill was such that he could make lebkuchen
fit to be eaten by the German portion of the saints
in Paradise.   At the end of three months the feelings of these young people towards each other were
quite clearly defined in their own minds; at the end
of six months, as they were sitting together one afternoon in the little back room at a time when the
shop happened to be empty, things came to the pleasing crisis that they both for a considerable period
had foreseen.

But then, unfortunately, came a storm—that neither of them had foreseen at all—that shook the
Café Nürnberg to its very foundations!

Gottlieb was the storm, and he moved over a wide

area with great rapidity and violence. He was central, naturally, over Hans and Minna : the first of
whom, after being denounced with great energy as
a viper who had been warmed to the biting point,
was ordered to take himself off without a single instant's delay, and never to darken the doors of the
Café Nürnberg again ; and the second of whom was
declared to be a baby fool, who must be kept locked
up in her own third-story back room, and fed on
nothing more appetizing than pumpernickel and water until she came to her senses. In the outer edges
of the storm the apprentices and the young men
who drove the wagons found themselves most hotly
involved ; and a very violent gust swept down upon
Aunt Hedwig and Herr Sohnstein, who surely were
as innocent in the premises as any two people quite
satisfactorily engaged in earnest but somewhat dila-
tory love-making of their own very well could be.
Indeed, this storm was an ill wind that blew a famous blast of luck to Herr Sohnstein : for Aunt Hedwig, being dreadfully upset by her brother's out-
break, went of her own accord to Herr Sohnstein
for sympathy and consolation—and found both in
such liberal quantities, and with them such tender
pleadings to enter a matrimonial haven where storms
should be unknown, that presently, smiling through
her tears, she uttered the words of consent for which
the excellent notary had waited loyally through
more than a dozen weary years. It was Herr Sohnstein's turn to be upset then. He couldn't believe,
until he had soothed himself with a phenomenal

number of pipes, that happiness so perfect could be real.

Possibly one reason why Gottlieb's storm was so violent was that he could not give any good reason for it. Hans really was a most estimable young man ; he came of a good family ; as a baker he was nothing short of a genius. All this Gottlieb knew, and all this he frequently had said to Aunt Hedwig and to Herr Sohnstein, and, worst of all, to Minna. As each of these persons now pointed out to him, in order to be consistent in his new position he must eat a great many of his own words ; and he would have essayed this indigestible banquet willingly had he been convinced that thus he really could have proved that Hans was a viper and all the other unpleasant things which he had called him in his wrath. In truth, Gottlieb was, and in the depths of his heart he knew that he was, neither more nor less than a dog in the manger. His feeling simply was that Minna was his Minna, and that neither Hans nor anybody else had any right to her. This was not a position that admitted of logical defence ; but it was one that he could be ugly and stick to : which was precisely what he did.

Minna did not remain long a prisoner in her own room, feeding upon pumpernickel and water and bitter thoughts. Aunt Hedwig and Herr Sohnstein succeeded in putting a stop to that cruelty. And these elderly lovers, whose fresh love had made them of a sudden as young as Minna herself, and had filled them with a warm sympathy for her, laid their heads together and sought earnestly to circumvent in her interest her father's stern decree. It was a joy to see this picture, in the little room back of the shop, of middle-aged love-making; and it was a little startling to find how the new youth that their love had given them had filled them with a quite extravagantly youthful recklessness. Herr Sohnstein, who was well known as a grave, sedate, and unusually cautious notary, seriously suggested (though he did not explain exactly how this would do it) that they should make an effort to bring Gottlieb to terms by burning down the bakery. And Aunt Hedwig, whose prudent temperament was sufficiently disclosed in the fact that she had hesitated in the matter of her own love affair for upward of a dozen years, not less seriously advanced the proposition that they all should elope from the Café Nürnberg and set up a rival establishment! Herr Sohnstein did not make any audible comment upon this violent proposal of Aunt Hedwig's, but it evidently put an idea into his head.

As Gottlieb happened to be walking along the south side of Tompkins Square, a fortnight or so after the tempest, he found his steps arrested by a great sign that lay face downward on trestles across the sidewalk, in readiness for hoisting in place upon the front of a smart new shop. Inside the shop he saw painters and paper-hangers at work; and on the large plate-glass window a man was gluing white letters with a dexterous celerity. The letters already in place read "Nürnberger Lebku—" And as to this

legend he saw "chen" added, he rolled out a stout
South German oath and stamped upon the ground.
But far stronger was the oath that he uttered as the
big sign was swung upward, and he read upon it, in
golden German letters:

ᵂürnberger Bäkerei.
Hans Kuhn.

That the Recording Angel blotted out with his
tears the fines which he was compelled on this occasion to record against Gottlieb Brekel in Heaven's
high chancery is highly improbable. In the only
known case of such lachrymic erasure the provoca-
tion to profanity was a commendable moral motive
that was eminently unselfish. But when Gottlieb
Brekel swore roundly in his native German all the
way from the south-west corner of Tompkins Square
to the corner of Third Street and the Bowery; and
from that point, when he had transacted his business there, all the way back to the Café Nürnberg
in Avenue B, his motives could not in any wise be
regarded as moral, and selfishness lay at their very
root.

Gottlieb already found himself involved in serious
difficulties with the many customers who bought his
lebkuchen; for with the departure of Hans he had
been compelled to fall back upon his own resources,
and with the most lamentable results. Great quantities of his first baking were returned to him, with
comments in both High German and Low German

of a very uncomplimentary sort.   His second baking
—saving the relatively inconsiderable quantities con-
sumed by the omnivorous children of St. Bridget's
School — simply remained upon his hands unsold.
And now, to make his humiliation the more complete, here was his discharged assistant setting up
as his rival; and with every probability that the attempted rivalry would be crowned with success.
Really there was something, perhaps, to be said in
palliation of Gottlieb's profanity after all.

When he told at home that evening of Hans
Kuhn's upstart pretensions, his statements were received with an ominous silence.   Aunt Hedwig only
coughed slightly, and continued her knitting with
more than usual energy.   Herr Sohnstein only moved
a little in his chair and puffed a little harder than
usual at his pipe.   Minna, who was in her wire cage
in the shop settling her cash, only bent more in-
tently over her books.   But when Gottlieb went a
step further and said, looking very keenly at Herr
Sohnstein as he said it, that some great rascal must
have lent Hans the money to make his fine start,
Aunt Hedwig at once bristled up and said with
emphasis that rascals, neither great nor small, were
in the habit of lending their money to deserving
young men ; and Herr Sohnstein, a little sheepishly
perhaps, and mumbling a little in his gray mustache,
ventured the statement that this was a free country
already, and people living in it were at liberty to
lend their money to whom they pleased ; and Minna,
looking up from her books — Gottlieb's back was

turned towards her—blew a most unfilial kiss from
the tips of her chubby fingers to Herr Sohnstein
right over her father's shoulder. All of which goes
to show that something very like open war had broken out in the Café Nürnberg, and that the once
united family dwelling therein was fairly divided
into rival camps.

Gottlieb's dreary case was made a little less dreary
when he found that the lebkuchen which Hans produced in his fine new bakery was distinctly an in-
ferior article; not much better, in fact, than Gottlieb's own. To any intelligent baker the reason for
this was obvious: Hans was making his lebkuchen
with new honey-cake. Thus made, even by the best
of recipes, it could not be anything but a failure.
Gottlieb gave a long sigh of relief as he realized
this comforting fact, and at the same time thought
of his own great store of honey-pots — there were
hundreds of them now—all ready and waiting to his
hand. But his feeling of satisfaction passed quickly
to one of impotent rage as he recognized his own
powerlessness, for all his wealth of honey-pots, to
make lebkuchen which would be eaten by anybody
but the tough-palated children from St. Bridget's
School. He was alone, smoking, in the little room
back of the shop as this bitter thought came to him;
in his rage he struck the table beside him a blow so
sounding that the family cat, peacefully slumbering
behind the stove, sprang up with a yell of terror and
made but two jumps to the open door. Coming on
top of all his other trials—the revolt of his own

13

little Minna, the defection of Aunt Hedwig, and the almost open enmity of Herr Sohnstein — this compulsory surrender of all his hope of honest fame was indeed a deadly blow.

Gottlieb smoked on in sullen anger; his heart torn and tortured, and his mind filled with a confusion of bitter evil thoughts. And presently—for the devil is at every man's elbow, ready to take advantage of any sudden weakness, or turn to his own purposes any too great strength—these thoughts grew more evil and more clear: until they fairly resolved themselves into the determination to steal from Hans the recipe for making lebkuchen, and so to crush completely his rival and at the same time to make certain his own fortune and fame.

Of course the devil did not plant the notion of theft in Gottlieb's mind in this bald fashion; for the devil is a most considerate person, and ever shows a courteous disposition to spare the feelings of those whom he would lead into sin. No: the temptation that he suggested was the subtle and ingenious one that Gottlieb should proceed to recover his own stolen property! His logic was admirable: Hans had been Gottlieb's assistant; and as such Gottlieb had owned him and his recipe as well. When Hans went away and took the recipe with him, he took that which still belonged to his master. Therefore, triumphantly argued the devil, Gottlieb had a perfect right to regain the recipe either by fair means or by foul. And finally, as a bit of supplementary devil-logic, the thought was

suggested that inasmuch as Hans certainly must
know the recipe by heart, the mere loss of the paper
on which it was written would not be any real loss
to him at all! It is only fair to Gottlieb's good
angel to state that during this able presentment of
the wrong side of the case he did venture to hint
once or twice—in the feeble, perfunctory sort of
way that unfortunately seems to be characteristic
of good angels when their services really are most
urgently required—that the whole matter might be
compromised satisfactorily to all the parties in interest by permitting Hans to marry Minna, and by then
taking him into partnership in the bakery. And it
is only just to Gottlieb to state that to these faint-
hearted suggestions of his good angel he did not
give one moment's heed.

Now the devil is a thorough-going sort of a person, and having planted the evil wish in Gottlieb's
soul he lost no time in opening to him an evil way
to its accomplishment. When Hans, a stranger in
New York, had come to work at the Café Nürnberg, Gottlieb had commended him to the good
graces of a friend of his, a highly respectable little
round Brunswicker widow who let lodgings, and
in the comfortable quarters thus provided for him
Hans ever since had remained. In this same house
lodged also one of Gottlieb's apprentices — a loose
young fellow, for whose proper regulation the widow
more than once had been compelled to seek his
master's counsel and aid. In this combination of
circumstances, to which the devil now directed his

attention, Gottlieb saw his opportunity. It was easy
to make the widow believe that the loose young
apprentice had taken the short step from looseness
to crime, and that a suspicion of theft rested upon
him so heavily as to justify the searching of his
room; it was easy to make the widow keep guard
below while Gottlieb searched; and it was very easy
then to search, not for imaginary stolen goods in
the chest of the apprentice, but for that which he
himself wanted to steal from the chest of Hans
Kuhn. As to opening the chest there was no difficulty at all. Gottlieb had half a dozen Nürnberg
locks in his house, and he had counted, as the event
proved correctly, upon making the key of one of
these locks serve his turn. And in the chest, without any trouble at all, he found a leather wallet, and
in the wallet the precious recipe—written on parchment in old High German that he found very difficult
to read, and dated in Nürnberg in the year 1603.
Gottlieb was pale as death as he went down-stairs
to the widow; and his teeth fairly chattered as he
told her that he had made a mistake. He tried to
say that the apprentice was not a thief—but the word
dieb somehow stuck in his throat. Keen chills penetrated him as he almost ran through the streets to
his home. For the devil, who heretofore had been
in front of him and had only beckoned, now was behind him and was driving him with a right good-
will.

When he entered the room at the back of the shop,
where Minna was sewing, and where Herr Sohnstein,

with his arm comfortably around Aunt Hedwig's
waist, was smoking his long pipe, he created a stir
of genuine alarm. As Aunt Hedwig very truly
said, he looked as though he had seen a ghost. Herr
Sohnstein, of a more practical turn of mind, asked
him if he had been knocked down and robbed ; and
the word *beraubt* grated most harshly upon Gottlieb's ears. But what cut him most of all was the
way in which Minna—forgetting all his late unkind-
ness at sight of his pale, frightened face—sprang to
him with open arms, and with all the old love in her
voice asked him to tell her what had gone wrong.
Under these favoring conditions, Gottlieb's good
angel bestirred himself somewhat more vigorously,
and for a moment it seemed not impossible that
right might triumph over wrong. But the devil
bustled promptly upon the scene, and of course had
things all his own way again in a moment. It certainly is most unfortunate that good angels, as a
rule, are so weak in their angelic knees !

Gottlieb pushed Minna away from him roughly ;
addressed to Aunt Hedwig the impolite remark that
ghosts only were seen by women and fools; in a surly
tone informed Herr Sohnstein that policemen still
were plentiful in the vicinity of Tompkins Square ;
and then, having planted these barbed arrows in the
breasts of his daughter, his sister, and his friend,
sought the retirement of his own upper room. As he
left them, Minna buried her face in Aunt Hedwig's
capacious bosom and cried bitterly, and Aunt Hedwig also cried ; and Herr Sohnstein, laying aside

for the moment his pipe, put his arms protectingly around them both. They all were very miserable.

In the upper room, where the air seemed so stifling that he had to open the window wide in order to breathe, Gottlieb was very miserable too. He was fleeing into Tarshish, this temporarily wicked baker; and just as fell out in the case of that other one who fled to Tarshish, his flight was a failure: for this little world of ours is far too small to give any one a chance to run away from committed sin.

Gottlieb tried to divert his thoughts from his crime, and at the same time tried to reap its reward by studying the stolen recipe; but his attempt was not successful. The cramped letters, brown with age, on the brown parchment, danced before his eyes; and the quaint, intricate High German phraseology became more and more involved. He could make nothing of it at all. And the thought occurred to him that perhaps he never would be able to make anything of it—that, without losing any part of the penalty justly attendant upon his crime, the crime itself might prove to be, so far as the practical benefit that he sought was concerned, absolutely futile. As this dreadful possibility arose before his mind a faintness and giddiness came over him. The room seemed to be whirling around him ; life seemed to be slipping away from him; there was a strange, horrible ringing in his ears. He leaned forward over the table at which he was sitting and buried his face in his hands.

Then, possibly, Gottlieb fell asleep, though of this

he never felt really sure. What is quite certain
is that he saw, as clearly as he ever saw her in life,
his dear dead Minna; but with a face so sad, so reproachful, so full of piteous entreaty, that his blood
seemed to stand still, while a consuming coldness
settled upon his heart. He struggled to speak with
her, to assure her that he would repair the evil that
he had done, to plead for forgiveness; but, for all
his striving, no other words would come to his lips
save those which a little while before he had spoken
so roughly to poor Aunt Hedwig: "The only people who see ghosts are women and fools!"

And then, of a sudden, he found himself still
seated at the table, the brown parchment still spread
out before him, and the faint light of early morning
breaking into the room. The window was wide
open, as he had left it, and he was chilled to the
marrow; he had a shocking cold in the head; there
were rheumatic twinges in all his joints as he arose.
What with the physical misery arising from these
causes, and the moral misery arising from his sense
of committed sin, he was in about as desperately bad
a humor with himself as a man could be. He was
in no mood to make another effort to read the difficult German of the recipe, the cause of all his troubles.
The sight of it pained him, and he thrust it hurriedly into an old desk in which were stored (and these
also were a source of pain to him) several generations
of uncollected bills—practical proofs that the adage
in regard to the impossibility of simultaneously possessing cakes and pennies does not always hold good.

He locked the desk and put the key in his pocket; and then returned the key to the lock and left it there, as the thought occurred to him that the locking of this desk, that never in all the years that he had owned it had been locked before, might arouse suspicion. It seemed most natural to Gottlieb that his actions should be regarded with suspicion ; he had a feeling that already his crime must be known to half the world.

And before night it certainly is true that the one person most deeply interested in the discovery and punishment of Gottlieb's crime—that is to say, Hans Kuhn—did know all about it ; which fact would seem surprising, considering how skilfully Gottlieb had gone about his work, were it not remembered that his unwitting accessory had been the little round Brunswicker widow, and were it not known that little round widows—Brunswick born or born elsewhere — as a class are incapable of keeping a secret.

This excellent woman, to do her justice, had followed Gottlieb's orders to the letter.   He had warned her not to tell the loose apprentice that his chest had been searched ; and, so far as that apprentice was concerned, wild horses might have been employed to drag that little round widow to pieces—at least she might have permitted the wild horses to be hitched up to her—before ever an indiscreet word would have passed her lips.   But when Hans Kuhn, for whom she entertained a high respect, and for whom she had also that warmly friendly feeling which trig

middle - aged widows not seldom manifest towards
good-looking young men, came to her in a fine state
of wrath, and told her that his chest had been ran-
sacked (he did not tell her of his loss, for he had not
himself observed it), she did not consider that she
violated any confidence in telling him everything
that had occurred.   It was all a mistake, she said ;
the Herr Brekel had gone into the wrong room ; she
must set the matter right at once ; that bad young
man might be a thief, after all.   Hans felt a cold
thrill run through him at the widow's words.   But
he controlled himself so well that she did not sus-
pect his inward perturbation ; and she accepted in as
good faith his offer to inform the Herr Brekel of his
error as she did, a day later, his assurance that the
matter had been satisfactorily adjusted, and that the
innocence of the apprentice had been proved.

And then Hans returned to his violated chest, and
found that the dread which had assailed his soul was
founded in substantial truth—the recipe was gone !
In itself the loss of the recipe was no very great
matter, for he knew it by heart ; but that Gottlieb—
who had also a cellar full of rich old honey - cake—
should have gained possession of it was a desperate
matter indeed.   Here instantly was an end to the
hope of successful rivalry that Hans had cherished;
and with the wreck of his luck in trade, as it seemed
to him in the first shock of his misfortune, away in
fragments to the four winds of heaven was scattered
every vestige of probability that he would have luck
in love.   Being so suddenly confronted with a com-

pound catastrophe so overwhelming, even a bolder baker than Hans Kuhn very well might have been for a time aghast.

But as his wits slowly came together again Hans perceived that the game was not by any means lost, after all; on the contrary, it looked very much as though he had it pretty well in his own hands. Gottlieb was a thief, and all that was needed to complete the chain of evidence against him was his first baking of lebkuchen; for that as clearly would prove him to be in possession of the stolen recipe as what the widow could tell would prove that he had created for himself an opportunity to steal it. The most agreeable way of winning a father-in-law is not by force of threatening to hale him to a police court, but it is better to win him that way than not to win him at all, Hans thought; and he thought also that this was one of the occasions when it was quite justifiable to fight the devil with fire. So his spirits rose, and now he longed for, as eagerly as in the first moments of his loss he had dreaded, the production of such lebkuchen at the Café Nürnberg as would prove the proprietor of that highly respectable establishment to be neither more nor less than a robber.

Hans was both annoyed and surprised as time passed on and the " cakes succulent but damnatory " were not forthcoming from Gottlieb's oven. He himself went on making unsatisfactory lebkuchen of bad materials by a good formula, and Gottlieb continued to make unsatisfactory lebkuchen by a bad formula of the best materials. Orthodox German

palates found nothing to commend and much to rep-
robate in both results. This was the situation for
several weeks. Hans could not understand it at all.
The subject was a delicate one to broach to Minna
during their short but blissful interviews about dusk
in the central fastnesses of Tompkins Square, at
which interviews Aunt Hedwig winked and Herr
Sohnstein openly connived by keeping watch for
them against Gottlieb's possible appearance ; for
Hans had determined that until he had positive
proof to go upon he would keep secret, and most of
all from Minna, the dreadful fact of her father's
crime. Therefore did he remain in a state of very
harrowing uncertainty, with his plan of campaign
completely brought to a stand.

During this period a heavy cloud hung over the
Café Nürnberg. Gottlieb came fitfully to his meals ;
and when he did come, he ate almost nothing. Each
day he grew more and more morose ; each night,
when poor Aunt Hedwig was not kept awake by her
own sorrowful thoughts, her slumbers were broken
by hearing her brother pacing heavily the floor of
the adjoining room. In some sort he made up for
his loss of sleep at night by sleeping of an evening
in the little room back of the shop, falling into rest-
less naps (when he should have been restfully smoking his long pipe), from which he would wake with
a start and sometimes with a cry of alarm, and would
dart furtive horrified glances at Aunt Hedwig and
Herr Sohnstein : who were doing nothing of a horri-
fying nature, only sitting cozily close together, more

or less enfolded in each other's arms.   It was a little inconsiderate on the part of the lovers, and very
hard on Minna, this extremely open love - making ;
for Minna's love-making necessarily was by fitful
snatches amid the bleak desolations of Tompkins
Square.   They would try to comfort each other, she
and Hans, as they stood cheerlessly under the chill
lee of the music stand; but their outlook was a dreary
one, and their efforts in this direction were not
crowned with any great success.   Sometimes as
Minna came home again along the west side of the
square, and saw in Spengler's window the wreaths of
highly-artificial immortelles with the word " Ruhe "
upon them in vivid purple letters, she fairly would
fall to crying over the thought that until she should
become a fit subject for such a wreath there was
small chance that any real rest would be hers.

However, all this is aside from Gottlieb's horrified
looks as he waked from his troubled slumbers—looks
which would disappear as he became thoroughly
aroused, but only to return again after his next uneasy nap.   One day he startled Aunt Hedwig by
asking her if she believed in ghosts.   Remembering his severe words in condemnation of her casual
reference to these supernatural beings, it was with
some hesitation that she replied that she did.   Still
more to her surprise, Gottlieb turned away from her
hurriedly, yet not so hurriedly but that she saw a
strange, scared look upon his face, and in a low and
trembling voice replied : " And so do I !"

And now the fact may as well be admitted frankly

that a ghost was the disturbing element that was making Gottlieb's life go wrong; that, as there seemed
to be every reason to believe, was hurrying him towards the grave: for a middle - aged German who
refuses to eat, whose regular sleep forsakes him, and
who actually gives up smoking, naturally cannot be
expected to remain long in this world.

It was the ghost of his dead wife.   At first she
appeared to him only in his dreams, standing beside
the desk in which he had placed the stolen recipe for
making lebkuchen, and holding down the lid of that
desk with a firm but diaphanous white hand.   Presently she appeared to him quite as clearly in his
waking hours.   Her face still wore an expression at
once tender and reproachful; but every day the look
of tenderness diminished, while the look of reproach
grew stronger and more stern.   Each time that he
sought to open the desk that he might take thence the
recipe and make his crime a practical business success,
the figure assumed an air so terribly menacing that
his heart failed him, and he gave over the attempt.

This, then, was the all - sufficient reason why the
good lebkuchen that would have proved Gottlieb a
thief was not for sale at the Café Nürnberg; and this
was the reason why Gottlieb himself, broken down
by loss of food and sleep and by the nervous wear
and tear incident to forced companionship with an
angry ghost, was drawing each day nearer and nearer
to that dark portal through which bakers and all
other people pass hence into the shadowy region
whence there is no return.

Gottlieb Brekel never had been an especially pious man. As became a reputable German citizen, he had paid regularly the rent of a pew in the Church of the Redemptorist Fathers in Third Street; but, excepting on such high feasts as Christmas and Easter, he usually had been content to occupy it and to discharge his religious duties at large vicariously. Aunt Hedwig's bonnet invariably was the most brilliantly conspicuous feature of the entire congregation, just as the prettiest face in the entire congregation invariably was Minna's. But now that Gottlieb was confronted with a spiritual difficulty, it occurred to him that he might advantageously resort in his extremity to spiritual aid. He had no very clear notion how the aid would be given; he was not even clear as to how he ought to set about asking for it; and he was troubled by the conviction that in order to obtain it he must not only repent of his sin, but must make atonement by restitution—a possibility (for the devil still had a good grip upon him) that made him hesitate a long while before he set about purchasing ease for his conscience at so heavy a material cost. However, his good angel at last managed to pluck up some courage—it was high time—and, strengthened by this tardily given assistance, he betook himself in search of consolation within church walls.

The Church of the Redemptorist Fathers is a very beautiful church, and at all times—save through the watches of the night and through one mid-day hour—its doors stand hospitably open, silently inviting poor sinners, weary and heavy laden with their sins,

to enter into the calm of its quiet holiness and there
find rest. Tall, slender pillars uphold its vaulted
roof, in the groinings of which lurk mysterious shad-
ows. Below, a warm, rich light comes through the
stained-glass windows: whereon are pictured the
blessed St. Alphonsus Maria de Liguori, founder of
the Redemptorist Congregation, blessedly instruct-
ing the chubby-faced choristers; and the Venerable
Clement Hofbauer, "primus in Germania" of the
Redemptorists, all in his black gown, kneeling, pray-
ing no doubt for the outcast German souls for the
saving of which he worked so hard and so well; and
(a picture that Minna dearly loved) St. Joseph and
the sweet Virgin and the little Christ-child fleeing
together through the desert from the wrath of the
Judean king. And ranged around the walls on perches
high aloft are statues of various minor saints and of
the Twelve Apostles; of which Minna's favorite was
the Apostle Matthias, because this saint, with his
high forehead tending towards baldness, and his long
gray beard and gray hair, and his kindly face, and
even the axe in his hand (that was not unlike a baker's peel), made her think always of her dear father.
The pew that Gottlieb paid for so regularly, and so
irregularly occupied, was just beneath the statue of
this saint; which, however, gave Minna less pleasure
than would have been hers had not the next saint in
the row been the Apostle Simon with his dreadful
saw. It must have hurt so horribly to be sawed in
two, she thought. In the dusky depths of the great
chancel gleamed the white marble of the beautiful

altar, guarded by St. Peter with his keys and St. Paul with his naked two-edged sword; and above the altar was the dead Christ on Calvary, with His desolate mother and the despairing Magdalene and St. John the divine.

Into this beautiful church it was that Gottlieb, led thither by his good angel, entered; and the devil— raging in the terrible but impotent fashion that is habitual with devils when they see slipping away from their snares the souls which they thought to win to wickedness—of course was forced to remain outside. But what feelings of keen repentance filled this poor sinning baker's heart within that holy place, what good resolves came to him, what light and re- freshment irradiated and cheered his darkened, har- ried soul—all these are things which better may be suggested here than written out in full. For these things are so real, so sacred, and so beautiful with a heavenly beauty, that they may not lightly be used for decorative purposes in mere romance.

Let it suffice, then, to tell—for so is our poor human stuff put together that trivial commonplace facts often exhibit most searchingly the changes for good or for evil which have come to pass in our in- most souls—that Gottlieb, on returning to the Café Nürnberg, ate a prodigious dinner; and after his dinner, for the first time in a fortnight, smoked a thoroughly refreshing pipe.

Over his dinner and his pipe he was silent, mani- festing, however, a sort of sheepishness and constraint that were not less strange in the eyes of Aunt Hed-

wig and Minna than was the sudden revival of his
interest in tobacco and food. As he smoked, a pleasant thought came to him. When he had knocked
the ashes from his pipe he ordered Minna, surlily, to
bring him his hat and coat ; he must pay a visit to
that rascal Sohnstein, he said; and so went out. He
left the two women lost in wonder ; and Aunt Hedwig, because of his characterization of her dear
Sohnstein as a rascal, disposed to weep. And yet,
somehow, they both felt that the storm was breaking,
and that clear weather was at hand. There was nobody in the shop just then; and the two, standing
behind the rampart of freshly-baked cakes that was
high heaped up upon the counter, embraced each
other and mingled tears, which they knew—by rea·
son of the womanly instinct that was in them—were
tears of joy.

And that very evening the prophecy of happiness
that was in their joyful sorrow was happily fulfilled.

Gottlieb did not return to the Café Nürnberg until
after nine o'clock. With him came Herr Sohnstein.
They both were very grave and silent, yet both exhibited a most curious twinklesomeness in their eyes.
Neither Aunt Hedwig nor Minna could make anything of their strange mood; and Aunt Hedwig was
put to her trumps completely when she was sure that
she saw her brother—who was whispering to Herr
Sohnstein behind the pie-counter—poke the notary
in the ribs. As to the joint chuckle at that moment
of those two mysterious men there could be no doubt;
she heard it distinctly !

14

Still further to Aunt Hedwig's surprise, for the Café Nürnberg never was closed before ten o'clock, and usually remained open much later, Gottlieb himself began to put up the shutters; and when this work was finished he came back into the shop and locked behind him the double front door. Almost as he turned the key there was a knock outside, as though somebody actually had been waiting in the street for the signal that the closing of the shutters gave.

"Another rascal would come in already, Sohnstein," said Gottlieb, gruffly. "Open for him, but lock the door again. I must go up-stairs."

Gottlieb, with a queer smile upon his face, left the little back room; and a moment later Minna uttered a cry of surprise, as Herr Sohnstein unlocked the door and her own Hans entered the shop. What, she thought, could all these wonders mean? As for Aunt Hedwig, she had sunk down into her big arm-chair and her bright black eyes seemed to be fairly starting from her head.

Herr Sohnstein locked the door again, as he had been ordered to do, and then brought Hans through the shop and into the little back room. Hans evidently was not a party to the mystery, whatever the mystery might be. He looked at Minna as wonderingly as she looked at him, and he was distressingly ill at ease. But there was no time for either of them to ask questions, for as Hans entered the room from the shop, Gottlieb returned to it. In his hand Gottlieb held the brown old parchment on which the lebkuchen recipe was written ; the smile had left his face; he was very pale. For a moment there was an awkward pause. Then Gottlieb, trembling a little as he walked, crossed the room to where Hans stood and placed the parchment in his hands. And it was in a trembling, broken voice that Gottlieb said:

"Hans, a most wicked man have I been. But my dead Minna has helped me, and here I give again to thee what I stole from thy chest—I who was a robber." Then Gottlieb covered his face with his hands, and presently each of his bony knuckles sparkled with a pendant tear.

"My own dear father!" said Minna; and her arms were around him, and her head was pressed close upon his breast.

"My own good brother, thou couldst not be a thief!" said Aunt Hedwig ; and, so saying, clasped her stout arms around them both.

"My good old friend! all now is right again," said Herr Sohnstein ; who then affected to put his arms around the three, but really embraced only Aunt Hedwig. However, there was quite enough of Aunt Hedwig to fill even Herr Sohnstein's long arms; and he made the average of his one-third of an embrace all right by bestowing it with a threefold energy.

The position of Hans as he regarded this affectionately writhing group (that was not unsuggestive of the Laöcoon: with a new motive, a fourth figure, a commendable addition of draperies, and a conspicuous lack of serpents) would have been awkward under any circumstances ; and as the circumstances were sufficiently awkward to begin with, he was very much embarrassed indeed. To Aunt Hedwig's credit be it said that she was the first (after Minna, of course ; and Minna could not properly act in the premises) to perceive his forsaken condition.

"Come, Hans," said the good Hedwig, her voice shaken by emotion and the tightness of Herr Sohnstein's grip about her waist.

"Thou hadst better come, Hans," added Herr Sohnstein, jollily.

"*Wilt* thou come, Hans—and forgive me ?" Gottlieb asked.

But it was not until Minna said, very faintly, yet with a heavenly sweetness in her voice: "Thou *mayst* come, Hans!" that Hans actually came.

And then for a while there was such hearty embracing of as much of the other four as each of them could grasp that the like of it all for good-will and lovingness never had been seen in a bakery before. And Gottlieb's good angel exulted greatly; and the devil, who had lingered about the premises in the hope that even at the eleventh hour the powers of evil might get the better of the powers of good, acknowledged his defeat with a howl of baffled rage: and then fled away in a blue flame and a flash of lightning that made the waters of the East River (which stream he was compelled to wade, thanks to General Newton, who took away his stepping-stones) fairly hiss and bubble. And never did he dare. to

"But it was not until Minna said, very faintly, yet with a heavenly sweetness in her voice: 'Thou mayst come, Hans?' that Hans actually came."

show so much as the end of his wicked nose in the
Café Nürnberg again!

"But thou wilt not take from me this little one,
my daughter, Hans?" Gottlieb asked, when they
had somewhat disentangled themselves. "Thou
wilt come and live with us, and be my partner, and
together we will make the good lebkuchen once
more. Is it not so?"

Hans found this a trying question. He looked
at Herr Sohnstein, doubtfully. "Ah," said Herr
Sohnstein, "thou meanest that a very hard-hearted,
money-lending man has hired a shop for thee and
has made it the most splendid bakery and the finest
restaurant on all the East Side, eh? And thou art
afraid that this man, this old miser man, will keep
thee to thy bargainings, already?"

Hans gave a deprecating nod of assent.

"Well, my boy Hans," Herr Sohnstein continued,
with great good-humor, and sliding his arm well
around Aunt Hedwig's generous waist again as he
spoke—"well, my boy Hans, let me tell thee that
that bad old miser man is not one-half so bad as thou
wouldst think. Dost thou remember that when he
had a garden made upon the roof of that fine bakery,
and thou toldst to him that to make a garden there
was to waste his money, what he said? Did he not
say that if he made the garden God would send the
flowers? And when that fine sign was made with
'Nürnberger Bäkerei' upon it, and thou toldst to him
that to take that name of Nürnberg was not fair
to his old friend, did he not tell thee that with his

old friend he would settle that matter so that there should be no broken bones? For did he not know already that for these five years past it has been the wish of Gottlieb's heart to leave this old bakery—where his lease ends this very coming May—and to have just such a new fine bakery upon the Square as now you two together will have? Ah, this bad old miser man is not afraid but that his miser money will come back to him again; and he is not such a fool but that he had faith in his good friend Gottlieb, and knew that all would end well. And now, truly, all will be happiness: for Gottlieb, who has gained a good son, can spare to me this dear Hedwig, his sister, and he will come to church with us and see us all married in one bright day."

Aunt Hedwig looked up into Herr Sohnstein's face as he ended this long speech—not so fine, perhaps, as some of the speeches which he had delivered in the criminal courts, but much more moving and a great deal more geniune than the very best of them —and, with her eyes filling with happy tears, said to him: "And it is to thee that we owe it, this happiness!"

But Herr Sohnstein's face grew grave and his voice grew reverent as he answered : "It is not so, my Hedwig. We owe our happiness to the good God who has taken away the evil that was in our dear Gottlieb's heart." They all were very quiet for a little space, and upon the silence broke the sweet sound of the clock bell in the near-by church-tower.

When the last stroke had sounded Herr Sohnstein

spoke again, and in his customary jolly tone : " As for these young ones here, we will unlock the door and let them walk out and look for a little at the music - stand that they love so well in the Square. And Hedwig shall sit beside me while we smoke our pipes, Gottlieb, eh ?   It is a long time already, old friend, since thou and I have sat together and smoked our pipes."

AN IDYL OF THE EAST SIDE.

In the matter of raising canary - birds — at once strong of body and of note, tamed to associate with humanity on rarely friendly terms, and taught to sing with a sweetness nothing short of heavenly— Andreas Stoffel was second to none. And this was not by any means surprising, for he had been born (and for its saintly patron had been christened) close by the small old town of Andreasberg : which stands barely within the verge of the Black Forest, on the southern declivity of the Harz—and which, while famous for its mines, is renowned above all other cities for the excellence of the bird songsters which there and thereabouts are raised.

Canary - birds had been the close companions of this good Andreas through all the fifty years of his lifetime. They had sung their sweet song of rejoicing at his birth—when the storks had brought him one day, while his father was far underground at work in the mines, and was vastly well pleased, when he came home all grimy at night, to find what a brave boy God had sent him by these winged messengers. They had sung over his cradle as his mother, knitting, rocked it in the midst of the long patch of sunlight that came through the low, wide window of the *bauernhaus*—the comfortable home with high - peaked roof, partly thatched and partly shingled, and with great drooping eaves, that was nooked snugly on the warm southern slope of the Andreasberg beside a little stream.   They had sung him awake many and many a bright summer morning; and one of his tenderest memories of the time when he was a very little boy—and was put to bed, as little boys should be, at sundown—was of their faint, irregular, sleepy-headed chirpings and twitterings as they settled themselves to slumber on their perches for the night.

And when the time came that Andreas, grown to man's estate, being one-and-twenty years old, but not to man's strength, for he was small of stature and frail, was left lonely in the world — the good father killed by a rock-fall in the mines, and the dear mother thereafter pining away from earth, and so to the heaven that gave her husband back to her — it was his house-mates the birds who did their best to cheer him with their songs.   And presently, as it seemed to him, these songs began to tell of new happiness in a new home far away across the mountains and beyond the sea—in that distant America where already his father's brother dwelt, and whereof he had heard wonderful stories of splendors and of riches incalculable all his life long.   Indeed, the adventurous uncle had prospered amazingly in the twenty years of his American exile: rising, in due course, from the position of a young man of most promiscuous all work in a delicatessen shop in New York to the position of owner of the business, shop and all.

"*The comfortable home with high-peaked roof, partly thatched and partly shingled.*"

To go to a land where such things as this were possible seemed to Andreas most wise; and to be near
his uncle, and the aunt and cousins whom he had
never seen, his sole remaining kin, held out to him a
pleasant promise of cheer and comfort in his loneli-
ness.

But, in very truth, the sweet burden of the song
of his birds was not born of thoughts of mere commonplace family affection and commonplace worldly
wealth.   Far more precious than these was the motive of the music that Andreas listened to and understood, and yet scarcely would acknowledge, even
to himself; for in America it was that Christine now
had her home — and that which set his heartstrings
a-thrilling, as he listened to the song of his birds,
was the deep, pure melody of love.

They had been children together, he and Christine,
their homes side by side on the flanks of the Andreasberg; and when, three years before, she had
gone with her father and her mother on the long
journey westward, the heart of Andreas Stoffel had
gone with her, and only his body was left behind
among the mountains of the Harz.   And Christine
had dulled to him a little the keen edge of the sorrow of their parting by admitting that she left her
own heart in the place of the heart that she bore
away.

More than once had the rich uncle, owner of the
delicatessen shop in New York, written to urge that
his nephew — whose frailty of body made him unfit
to enter upon the hard life of a worker in the mines

—should come to America; and with his large knowledge of affairs the uncle had explained that the best
bill of exchange in which money could be carried
from Andreasberg to New York was canary-birds,
that could be bought for comparatively little in the
German town, and that would be worth in the American city a very great sum. And now on this shrewd
advice Andreas acted. The dear old *bauernhaus* was
sold, and its furnishing with it; and all the money
thus gained, together with the greater sum that, little by little, his father had added to the store in the
old leather bag (saving only what the journey would
cost) was spent in buying the finest canary - birds
which money could buy; so that for a long while
after that time Andreasberg was desolate, for all of
its sweetest singers were gone.

Thus it fell out that even in the time of his long
journey his birds still sang to him; and his fellow-
travellers by land and sea regarded curiously this
slim, pale youth, who shyly kept apart from human
converse and communed with his companions the
birds. And so lovingly well did Andreas care for
his little feathered friends that not one died throughout the whole long passage; and as the ship came
up the beautiful bay of New York on a sunny May
morning, while Andreas stood on the deck with his
cages about him, very blithely and sweetly did the
birds sing their hopeful song of greeting to the
New World.

But it was a false song of hope, after all. Hearts
were fickle thirty years ago, even as hearts are fickle

to-day; and the first news that Andreas heard when he was come to his uncle's home (a very fine home, over a very fine shop, indeed) was that Christine had been a twelvemonth married—in very complete forgetfulness of all her fine words about the heart left behind her, and of all her fine promises that she would be true!

That there be such things as broken hearts is an open question. Yet when this news came suddenly to Andreas a keen agony of pain went through his heart as though it were really breaking; and with his hands pressed tightly against his breast, and with a face as pale as death itself, he fell to the floor. He would have died then very willingly; and it was very unwillingly—the fierce pain leaving him as suddenly as it had come — that he returned to life. Whatever may be said for or against the probability of broken hearts, there can be no question as to the verity of broken lives. That day, assuredly, the life of Andreas Stoffel was broken, and it never wholly mended again. For a while even the song of his birds lost all its sweetness, and seemed to him but a discordant sound.

Yet even a broken life, until it be snuffed out entirely, must battle in the world for standing - room. Luckily for Andreas, there was no need for him to question how his own particular battle should be made. The shape in which his little store of worldly wealth was cast obviously determined the lines on which he should seek maintenance. It was plain that by the rearing and the selling of canary-birds he

must gain support until the time should come (and
he hoped that it would come soon) when he might
find release from this earth, where love so soon grows
false and cold.

The rich uncle, who was a kind-hearted man, gave
his help in the matter of finding a shop wherein the
canary - bird business might be advantageously carried on, and gave also the benefit of his commercial
wisdom and knowledge of American ways. And so,
with no great difficulty, Andreas was soon established in a snug little place of his own on the East
Side; where the friendly German speech sounded
almost constantly in his ears, and where the friendly German customs obtained almost as completely as
in his own dear German home. But, after all, the
change was a dismal one. As his unaccustomed nose
was assailed by the rank oil-vapors blown across
from Hunter's Point he longed regretfully for the
fresh, aromatic air that the south winds swept up
and over his old home from the pines of the Schwarzwald; and the contrast was a sorry one between a
home on the slopes of the Harz Mountains and a
home in Avenue B.

Yet had these been his only sorrows, and had he
borne them — as he had hoped to bear them — with
Christine, his lot would have been anything but hard.
It was the deep heart - wound that he had suffered
that made his life for many a year a very dreary
one; too dreary for him to find much pleasure even
in the singing of his birds. Now and again he met
Christine. At their first meeting—in his uncle's fine

parlor over the fine delicatessen shop, one Sunday
afternoon—she was, as she well might be, confused
in her speech and very shamefaced in her ways.
Her husband was with her, quite a prosperous person, so Andreas was told, who had built up a great
business in the pork and sausage line. He was a
loud-voiced, merry man; and he aired his wit freely,
though evidently with no intent to be unkind, upon
the lover out of whose lucklessness his own luck
had come. Even as pretty a girl as Christine could
not have more than one husband at a time, said this
big Conrad, with great good-humor; and so, since
they could not both marry her, Andreas would do
well to stop crying over spilled milk. They all would
be very good friends, he added, and Andreas would
be godfather to the first child. He put out his big
hand as he made this proffer of friendship; and although Andreas could not refuse to clasp it, there
was not, in truth, any great store of friendliness for
Christine's loud-voiced husband in his heart. So soon
as this was possible, he was glad to get away from
the merry Sunday afternoon gathering in his uncle's
fine parlor to the more sympathetic society of his
birds. Yet there did not seem to him much music
in the singing of his birds that day.

Christine was vastly proud of her big, rosy-faced,
noisy husband, whose sausage-making greatly prospered, and to whom the American dollars rolled in
bravely. But even in these days of her good-luck
she sometimes found herself thinking—when Conrad's rough love-making was still further rough-

15

ened, and his noisiness greatly increased, by too free draughts of heady German beer — of the gentler ways and constant tenderness of her earlier lover, whose love, with her own promise to be true to it, she had so lightly cast aside. Thoughts of this sort, it is true, did not often trouble her, but now and then they gave her a little heart-pang; and the pang would be intensified, sometimes, as the thought also would come to her that perhaps it was because she had broken her plighted troth that her many prayers to become a mother remained unanswered.

As time went on, Christine's sorrows came to be of a more instant sort. Her too jolly husband's fondness for heady beer grew upon him, and with its increase came a decrease in the success that until then had been attendent upon his sausage - making. His business fell away from him by degrees into soberer and steadier hands, which had the effect of making him take to stronger drinks than beer in order that he might the more effectually forget his troubles. He lost his merriness, and somewhat of his loudness, and became sullen; and the wolf always was shrewdly near the door. Thus, in a very bad way indeed, things went on for half a dozen years; then the big Conrad, what with drink and worry, fell ill—so ill, that for a long while he lay close to the open jaws of Death.

No one ever knew — though several people quite accurately guessed—why the wolf did not fairly get into the house during that dismal time. It is certain that when Conrad arose from his bed at last, a

thin remnant of his former bigness, there were few
high-priced birds left in Andreas Stoffel's little shop,
where there had been a score or more when his sickness began.   And, possibly, it was something more
than a mere coincidence that nearly all of the few
which remained were sold about the time that Conrad started again, in a very humble way, his business of sausage-making.

But if Andreas did thus sacrifice his birds for
Christine's good, he did not grudge the sacrifice ; for
upon the big Conrad poverty and sickness had exer-
cised a chastening and most wholesome influence.
He got up out of his bed a changed man ; and the
change, morally at least, was greatly for the better.
Physically the result was less salutary ; indeed, he
never quite recovered from his sharp attack ; and
three or four years later, just as his business was
getting into good shape again, he sickened suddenly,
and then promptly paid to nature the debt that all
men owe, and that his partial return to health had
but a little time delayed.

But Christine was not left desolate in the world,
for in the last year of her husband's life the strong
yearning that so possessed her had been satisfied,
and she was the mother of a baby girl.   Andreas,
claiming the fulfilment of the promise made so long
before, had stood godfather to the little Rosa—for
so, because of her fresh rosiness, was she named; and
there was a strange, sorrowful longing in his heart
when, the rite being ended, he came again to his
lonely home and sat him down to be comforted by

the singing of his birds : for while the children of
Alice call Bartram father, there must be ever a
weary weight of sadness in the world.

Life had not given so much of happiness to Christine—though, possibly, her happiness was equal to
her deserts—that her hold upon life was a very firm
one ; and although she tried, for the little Roschen's
sake, to put fresh strength into her grasp, the pressure of poverty and care and sorrow all combined to
make her loosen it.   Gently, a little at a time, her
hold gave way. She knew what was coming, and so
did Andreas.   Once or twice they spoke about it ;
and spoke also of the old days on the Andreasberg,
when began the love that in one of their hearts at
least never had grown cold. And for this old love's
sake Andreas promised that when she was gone the
little Roschen should find a home with him and with
his birds.   It was not a great while after this promise was made that the end came.

Some of the women laughed a little, and cried a
little too, when, after the funeral, old Andreas—for
so already had they begun to call him, because of
his silent habit and quaint, old - fashioned ways—
asked to be shown how a baby should be carried ;
and, being in this matter properly instructed, bore
away with careful tenderness in his arms the little
Roschen to her new home. And when he was
come home with her, the birds, as though in welcome—which seemed the more real because certain of the tamer ones among them came forth
from their open cages and perched upon his arm—

"And when he was come home with her, the birds broke forth together into a chorus of sweetest song."

broke forth together into a chorus of sweetest song.

The good-wives living thereabouts were somewhat shocked at the thought of risking a baby's life in the care of a man who was qualified only to minister intelligently to the needs of baby canary-birds; yet were they not a little touched when they came—in unnecessary numbers, as Andreas thought—to give him the benefit of their superior wisdom in the premises by finding how well, in a queer, awkward way, he was discharging the duties of his office; and such gentleness in a man they all vowed that they had never seen. Yet it was not surprising that his quaint effort was crowned with so signal a success; as the birds could have explained, had their song-notes been rendered into human speech, Andreas had served an apprenticeship in caring for them which well fitted him to care with a mother's tenderness for this little girl, who, such was his love for her, seemed to him in all verity to be his own proper child. Benefiting by the advice which so lavishly was bestowed upon him, he presently became—as even the most critical of the women were forced to admit—a much better mother to the little Roschen than many a real mother might have been. It was, indeed, a sight worth travelling far to see, this of Andreas washing and dressing the baby in the sunny room at the back of the shop where hung the cages in which were the choicest of his birds. Roschen's first conscious memory was of laughing and splashing in her little tub in the sunshine, while all around her was a carolling of song.

In the course of the years which had drifted by since Andreas came with his birds to New York that May morning he had not made for himself many friends. To be a friend of birds a man must have a quiet habit of body, and great gentleness of nature, and a true tenderness of heart; which qualities tend also to solitariness, being for the most part harmed rather than fostered by association with mankind. As suited him well, his business was not one that called him much abroad, nor that brought him greatly into contact with his fellows. In his good care the famous stock of songsters which he had brought with him from the fatherland had increased prodigiously; and even the sale of nearly all his best old birds, about the time that Conrad was ill, had worked, in the long run, to his benefit; for he had taken these birds to one and another of the great dealers, who thus came to know that in the little shop on Avenue B were to be found canaries the like of which for tameness and for rare beauty of note could not be bought elsewhere in all New York. Thereafter, as his young birds grew up, learning from Andreas himself the lesson of gentleness, and from his teaching-birds the lesson of sweetness of note, he had no lack of high-paying customers; so that from his business he derived an income far in excess of his modest needs. What went with the overplus was known only to certain of his country-folk, whose ill venture after greater fortune in America had proved to be but a fiercer struggle with still greater poverty than they had struggled with at home ; and no doubt the angels also kept track of his modest benefactions, for such is reputed to be their way.

Many a wounded life was healed by these hidden ministrations on the part of Andreas; and, as rightly followed, great love there was for him in many a humble heart. But love of this sort is not friendship, for friendship requires some one plane at least of equality, and also association and converse, which conditions were lacking in the case of Andreas and those to whom he gave his aid ; for the shyness of his nature led him to keep himself apart—save when the demand upon his charity was for that comfort and sympathy which can only be given in person— from those whose burdens he lightened ; so that, for the most part, while the needed help was given the hand that gave it remained concealed.

Yet with a few of his country-folk in New York Andreas had established, in course of time, relations of warm friendliness. Of his kin only two cousins were left ; for the rich, good uncle, from overmuch eating of his own delicatessen, had come to a bilious ending ; and his uncle's widow, wise in her generation, had returned to her native town in Saxony, where she was enabled, by reason of the fortune that the delicatessen - shop had brought to her, to outshine the local baroness, and presently to attain the summit of her highest hopes and happiness by wedding an impoverished local baron, and so becoming a baroness herself. Her two sons were well pleased with this marriage. They were carrying on a great business in hog products, and had purchased for themselves fine estates in the country and fine houses in town. To be able to speak of their mother as "the baroness" suited them very well. Andreas saw but little of these gilded relatives—who yet were good-hearted men, and very kindly disposed towards him—for their magnificent surroundings were appalling to his simple mind. His few friends were more nearly in his own walk in life, and his friendship with them had been built up, as substantial friendship should be, by slow degrees.

At the Café Nürnberger, near by his own little shop—a bakery celebrated for the excellence of its bread, and for the great variety of its toothsome German cakes—it was his custom to make daily purchases. With the plump, rosy Aunt Hedwig, who presided over the bakery, he passed the good word of the day shyly; he responded shyly to the friendly nod of the baker, Gottlieb Brekel, when that worthy chanced to be in the shop; and he shyly greeted a certain jolly Herr Sohnstein, a German lawyer of distinction, who was about the bakery a great deal and who popularly was believed to be a suitor for the plump Hedwig's plump hand. And these shy greetings might have gone on day after day for all eternity—or at least for so much of it as these several persons were entitled to live out on earth—without increasing one particle in cordiality, had there not been one other dweller in the bakery to act as a solvent upon the bird-dealer's reserve. This was the baker's daughter Minna, a child a year or two older than Roschen and cast in a sturdier mould.

There was that about Andreas which drew all children to him, even as his birds were drawn to him; and a part of the spell certainly was the love for children that always was in his heart. The small Minna was disposed not a little to caprice—for she was a motherless child, and Aunt Hedwig humored her waywardness a trifle more than was good for her—and she manifested, usually, a certain haughtiness towards those who sought to make friends with her. Yet of her own accord one day, when Andreas had ceased to be a stranger to her, she went up to him and offered him a kiss. Aunt Hedwig volubly explained to Andreas the honor that had been done him, and from that moment was disposed herself to be most friendly with him—as was also the baker, and as was also Herr Sohnstein, when the story of this extraordinary performance duly was related to them. And thus there began a real friendship between Andreas and these kindly souls that ever grew riper as the years went on. Sometimes of an evening, when his birds were all asleep and he was left lonely, Andreas would step around to the bakery; and would sit for an hour or so in the little room back of the shop, listening pleasantly to the talk of Gottlieb and Herr Sohnstein, as they smoked their long pipes, and even laughing in a quiet way at the merry sallies thrown into the conversation by Aunt Hedwig as she sat knitting beside the fire. Andreas himself rarely spoke—it was not his way; but there was such a sympathetic quality in his silence that his lack of words passed almost unobserved. Much more attention was attracted by the fact that he did not smoke—a fact that was looked upon as most extraordinary. But this also went unheeded after a while, as it well might in a small room wherein Gottlieb and Herr Sohnstein were smoking with such vigor that the air was a deep, heavy blue. It was because his birds did not like smoke that he had given up his pipe, he explained, simply; and only to Minna did it occur to say, after she had turned the matter over in her small mind for a while, that the Herr Stoffel must be a very kind-hearted man to go without smoking because the smell of tobacco-smoke wasn't nice for his birds.

When Andreas took the little Roschen to his home, that sad day after the funeral, the good Hedwig was among the first of the womenkind to go to him with tenders of instruction and advice; for while Hedwig was only, as it were, a matron by brevet, she was deeply impressed by the extent of her own knowledge in the matter of how motherless children should be raised; and it is but just to add that this self-confidence was fully warranted by the good results that had attended upon her care of her brother's child. Something of the story of Andreas and Christine, and something of what he had done for her and for her husband, was known in the bakery; and enough more was guessed to make these friends of his feel towards him, because of it all, a still stronger and more earnest friendship. Herr Sohnstein, who, being a lawyer with an extensive practice in the criminal courts, was not by any means in the habit of praising his fellow-men indiscriminately, even went so far as to say that Andreas was "better than any of the saints already." And when Aunt Hedwig, somewhat shocked at this comparison to the disfavor at a single thrust of the whole body of saints put together, reproved Herr Sohnstein for his irreverence, he stoutly declared that while his knowledge of saints was comparatively limited—since they did not come within the jurisdiction of the courts— he certainly never had read of one who had shown a finer quality of charity, both in forgiveness and in self-sacrifice, than that which Andreas had displayed.

"Don't you make believe, Hedwig," Herr Sohnstein continued, "that if you go off after promising yourself to me and marry another fellow, that I'll take care of him when he's sick, and set him up in business when he gets well, and wind up by giving him a first-class funeral; and don't you get it into your head that I'm going to adopt any of your children that are not mine too—for I'm not a saint already, even if Andreas is."

To which general declaration Aunt Hedwig replied, with much spirit, that in the first place Herr Sohnstein had better wait until she promised to marry him—or to marry anybody, for that matter— before he took to preaching to her; that in the second place it was unnecessary for him to declare that he was not a saint, since only a deaf blind man would be likely to take him for one; and that in the third place he would do well to save his breath to cool his broth: at which lively sally they all laughed together very comfortably.

With these good friends Andreas consulted in all important matters relating to Roschen's well-being. Aunt Hedwig's practical advice in regard to clothing and food and general care-taking was of high value in the early years; and it was Gottlieb's suggestion, when the time came for beginning the sowing of seeds of wisdom in her small mind, that Roschen should go with his own Minna to the school where the Sisters taught; and of a Sunday the children went also together to be instructed by the Redemptorist Fathers in the way of godliness. So these little ones grew in years and in knowledge and in grace together, and towards each other they felt a sisterly love.

Insensibly, too, as Roschen grew out of childhood into girlhood, her attitude towards her adoptive father changed. In the great matters of her life he still cared for her, planning always for her good, and withholding from her nothing suited to her station in life that money could buy. In the matter of her music, Aunt Hedwig declared that he was positively extravagant; yet accepted in good part his excuse that a voice so beautiful deserved to be well trained. It was her mother's voice alive again, he said; and as he spoke, Aunt Hedwig saw that there were tears in his eyes. But while Andreas still continued the larger of his parental duties, in the smaller matters of every-day life his adopted daughter

"And of a Sunday the children went together to be instructed by the Redemptorist Fathers."

now cared for him ; so beginning to pay the debt
(though to neither of them, such was their love for
each other, did any thought of debt or of payment
ever occur) that she owed him for all his goodness
to her and to her dead father and mother in the past.

In truth, it was a pretty sight to see Roschen first
beginning to play at keeping house for her father—
for so she always called him—and then, in a little
while, keeping house for him most excellently in real
earnest.   Here, again, the good qualities of Aunt
Hedwig came to the front, for to her intelligent direction was due the rather surprising success that
attended Roschen's ambitious attempt to become so
early a *hausfrau.*   Time and again was a great culinary disaster averted by a rapid dash on Roschen's
part from her imperilled home to the bakery, where
Aunt Hedwig's advice was quickly obtained and then
was promptly acted upon.   And if sometimes the advice came too late to avert the catastrophe—as on
that memorable and dreadful day when Roschen
boiled her sausage-dumplings without tying them in
a bag—the lessons taught by calamitous experience
caused only passing trouble, and tended, in the long-
run, to good.

Indeed, by the time that Roschen was sixteen years
old, and had so far passed through her apprenticeship that she no longer was compelled to make sudden and frantic appeals to Aunt Hedwig for aid, the
little household over which she presided so blithely
was very admirably managed ; and it certainly was
as quaint and as pretty an establishment as could be

found anywhere upon the whole round globe. Whoever entered the little shop was greeted with such a thrilling and warbling of sweet notes that all the air seemed quivering with music, and the leader of the bird choir was a certain wonderful songster that Andreas had named the Kronprinz, and for which he repeatedly had refused quite fabulous sums. Andreas himself had bred the Kronprinz, and had given him the education that now made him such a wonder among birds, and that made him also of such great value as an instructor of the young birds whose musical education was still to be gained. After his adopted daughter, Andreas held this bird, and justly, to be the most precious thing that he owned.

But far sweeter than the singing of the prized Kronprinz—at least, to any but a bird-fancier's ears —was the singing that usually was to be heard above the trilling of the canaries, and that came from the room at the back of the shop where Roschen was engaged in her housewifely duties. It was such music as the angels made, Andreas declared, yet thinking most of all of one angel voice, the memory of which while still on earth was very dear to him; and even in the case of those who were moved by no tender association of the sweet tones of the living and the dead this estimate of Roschen's singing did not seem unduly high. Gustav Strauss, the son of the great bird-dealer over in the rich part of the town, vowed that Andreas was entirely right in his angelic comparison; and Ludwig Bauer, the young shoemaker, who lived next door but one, went even

further, and said that Roschen's voice was as much
sweeter than any mere angel's voice as Roschen herself was sweeter and better than all the angels in
Paradise combined. There was nothing halting nor
half-way in Ludwig Bauer's opinion in this matter,
it will be observed.

The little room wherein Roschen sang so sweetly
while at her work was their kitchen and dining-room
and parlor all in one. As noon-time drew near there
would come out into the shop from this room, through
the open door-way, such succulent and enticing odors
of roasting pork and stewing onions and boiling cab-
bages, that even Bielfrak—as the Spitz dog, who was
chained as a guard close beneath the cage of the
Kronprinz, appropriately was named—would fall to
licking his chops as he hungrily sniffed these smells
delectable; and Andreas suddenly would discover
how hungry he was, and would make occasion to go
to the door-way that he might see if the setting of
the table was begun.

"Patience, father! Presently! You are as bad as
Bielfrak himself!" Roschen would say; and as this
attribution of gluttony to her father was a time-hon-
ored joke between them, they always would laugh
over it pleasantly. And then Andreas would stand
and watch his little *hausfrau* with a far-away look in
his gentle blue eyes as she bustled about her work
in the sunny room, her pretty dimpled arms bared
to above the elbow, her lovely cheeks (because of
much stooping over the fire) brighter even than the
roses after which she had been named, her golden

hair done up in a trig, tight knot (as Aunt Hedwig
had taught her was the proper way for hair to be arranged while cooking was going on), and over her
tidy print gown a great white apron, fashioned in an
ancient German shape, as guard against the splash-
ings and spillings which even the most careful of
cooks cannot always control. In the sunny windows, opening to the south, flowers were growing;
the Dutch clock, with pendulous weights made in
the similitude of pine-cones, ticked against the wall
merrily; Mädchen, the cat—who, being most prolific
of kittens, notoriously belied her name—sat bunched
up in exceeding comfort on a space expressly left
for her upon the sunny window - ledge among the
plants; steam arose in light clouds from the various
pots upon the stove, and in the middle of the little
room the table stood ready for the dinner to be
served.

It was a very cheerful, home - like picture this;
and yet many a time, as Andreas stood in the door-
way and contemplated it, there would be tears in his
eyes, and a strange feeling, half of glad thankfulness, half of very sorrowful longing, in his heart.
She was so like her dead mother! In look, in speech,
in motions of the body, in turns of the head, and in
gestures of the hands she was Christine over again.
Sometimes Andreas would forget his fifty years and
all the sorrows of hope destroyed and irrevocable
death-parting which his fifty years had brought him,
and would fancy for a moment that he was young
again, and that the dearest wish of his life was here

fulfilled. And then she would call him "Father!" and his moment's dream of happiness would die coldly in his heart. Yet would there come to him always an after - glow of solacing warmth, as comforting thoughts would steal in upon him of the happiness not a dream—different from that which he had hoped for in his youth, but most sweet and real—that God's goodness had given him in these his later years.

Andreas truly was old Andreas now. As men's lives go, his age was not great ; but sorrow had made him, as it had made many another man, far older than the mere number of years which he had lived. No great store of strength had been his at the beginning, and the heart-break that he had suffered that day of his landing in the New World, when faith and love and hope all died together at a single blow, was less a sentimental figure than a physical reality. A like pang, yet not so keen, had wrenched him when he first came to know of Christine's sharp trial of poverty, and another seized him in the night-time following that sad day when she passed away from earth. And now of late, without any cause at all, these pangs had come again. Andreas was glad that they had come always when he was alone ; for the pain was too searching to be wholly hidden, and his strong desire was that Roschen should be spared all knowledge of his suffering. In his own mind he perceived quite clearly what before long must come to pass. And it was a good happening, he thought, that in Gottlieb Brekel and Aunt Hedwig, and the excellent Herr Sohnstein, who, being a lawyer, could

16

care well for the little store in the bank and for the
little house that Andreas now owned, Roschen had
such stanch and worthy friends. The only signs of
these thoughts which Roschen perceived was that
her father grew much keener in the matter of selling
his birds at high prices; and that she was somewhat seriously reproved when, in her housekeeping
or in her occasional expeditions to the fine shops in
Grand Street, she ventured upon any small extrav-
agance. But Roschen would laugh when thus reproved, and would declare that her father, who long
had been a glutton, was become a miser already in
his old age; whereat Andreas also would laugh, yet
not quite so heartily as Roschen liked to hear him
laugh when she cracked her little jokes upon him,
and would say that sometimes a miser was not
thought by his heirs so bad a fellow when they
found what a snug little fortune he had left behind
him all safe in the bank.

It was because of these thoughts, which he kept
hidden from her, that Andreas began to take a much
more active interest in what Roschen had to say
from time to time about certain young men of her acquaintance. The young man of whom she spoke most
frequently, and with a frank friendliness, was the
handsome young assistant baker at the Café Nürnberger; a very capable young fellow, Hans Kuhn
by name, who of late had brought that excellent
bakery into great vogue because of the almost mirac-
ulously good lebkuchen which he baked there. But
Andreas was not at all alarmed by this open friend-

ship; for Hans and the stout Minna Brekel were to
be married presently, and Roschen's feeling obviously was no more than hearty good-will towards the
lover of her dear sister-friend. Fine chatterings she
and Minna had, as Andreas inferred from her occasional brief reports of them, about the prodigious
matrimonial event that was so near at hand. As
Andreas also inferred, these chatterings put various notions of an exciting and somewhat disturbing
sort into Roschen's little head. If one young girl
might get married, so might another, no doubt she
thought; and it is conceivable that from this mental statement of a rational abstract possibility her
thoughts may have passed on to consideration of the
concrete possibilities involved in her own relations
with the good-looking Gustav Strauss, son of the
rich bird-dealer, or with the good-looking young
shoemaker, Ludwig Bauer, who lived next door but
one.

It is certain that when Roschen had arrived at
the dignity of eighteen years, and her hitherto slim
figure had taken on quite a plump, pleasing womanly roundness, the business visits of the young Herr
Strauss to the little bird shop on the East Side became, as it struck Andreas, rather curiously frequent.
And about this time, also, their neighbor Ludwig developed a very extraordinary interest in the business
of raising canary-birds. It was a business that he
long had thought of engaging in, he explained; and
he truly did exhibit an aptitude in comprehending
and in practising its mysteries that greatly exalted

him in the little bird-dealer's esteem.   The birds all
seemed to recognize a friend in him ; and even those
which were but partially tamed, and were gentle
only with Andreas himself, would perch willingly
upon his hand.   With Andreas it long had been a
maxim that canary-birds were rare judges of human
character, and the testimonial thus given to Ludwig's worth counted with him for a great deal—as
did also the quite converse opinion of the birds in
regard to the young Herr Strauss: from whom, notwithstanding his training in the care of their kind,
they always flew away, and whose mere presence in
the shop sufficed to make every bird ruffle himself
and to chirp angrily in his cage.   Yet Herr Strauss
was most agreeable in his manners, and was a very
personable young man.   As for his riches, they
spoke for themselves in his fine attire and in his fine
gold watch and chain ; and he also spoke for them,
making frequent allusions to his comfortable present
position in the world as his father's partner, and to
his still more comfortable prospective position as his
father's sole heir.

Ludwig, on the other hand, could not boast of
any great amount of gilding upon, as Andreas believed it to be, the sterling metal of which he was
made.   But he was by no means what would be considered by the dwellers on the East Side a poor man.
He was a steady and a good master-workman, with
three or four apprentices under him ; and all day
long there was to be heard in his shop the cheerful,
business-like sound of the thumping of short ham-

mers on lap-stones, together with the loud clicking
of the sewing-machine on which the delicate stitch-
ing of uppers was done. In the window, screened
with a green curtain of growing vines — as is the
pretty custom with most of the German shoemakers
on the East Side—there always might be seen a pair
or two of well-made stout shoes drying in the sunshine on their lasts ; and with these a half-dozen
or more pairs of shoes newly soled and heeled in a
substantial, workmanlike fashion that would have
done credit to Hans Sachs himself. Making and
mending together, it was a very good business that
Ludwig was doing ; each year a better balance was
lodged to his credit in the savings - bank, and the
great golden boot that hung above his door-way told
no more than the truth of the good work that was
done and of the good money that was well earned
within. From the stand-point of public opinion on
the East Side, this thriving young shoemaker already was a man of substance, whose still more substantial future was assured.

There was in the nature of Ludwig much the same
simplicity and gentleness that characterized Andreas
—which common qualities, no doubt, had much to
do with the strong friendship that there was between them; and all his neighbors, remembering
how good a son he had been, and knowing also how
deeply he still sorrowed for the dear mother lost to
him in death, were more than ready to vouch for the
goodness of his heart. Indeed, it was while trying
to comfort him a little after this great sorrow fell

upon him that Roschen first felt towards him something more than the passing interest that every maiden reasonably feels in every seemly young man. Her disposition towards him, to be sure, even when thus stimulated by a sympathetic melancholy, was only that of friendliness; but it evidently was a friendliness so cordial and so sincere that it made quite a tolerable foundation upon which Ludwig freely built fine air-castles of hope. For his disposition towards Roschen was altogether that of a lover —as anybody might have known after hearing that decided expression of his opinion to the effect that all the angels singing together could not make music so sweet as the music of her voice.

In due time, in accordance with the decorous German custom, both of these young men made formal application to Andreas for permission to be ranked formally as Roschen's suitors; and, as it chanced, they both preferred their requests upon the same day. The young Herr Strauss undeniably had some strong points to make in his own favor; and he made them, to do him justice, without any hesitation or false modesty. As he truly said—speaking with an easy assurance, and airily fingering his gold watch-chain as he spoke—in marrying him Roschen would make an excellent match. In rather marked contrast with this justifiable yet not wholly pleasing assumption of self-importance, was the modest tone in which Ludwig urged his suit; yet was Andreas not unfavorably impressed by the fact that he dwelt less upon his deserts than upon his desire to be deserv-

ing ; and that in connection with the creditable presentment that he made of the condition of his worldly affairs he did not insist, as the Herr Strauss had
insisted, upon a minute examination of Roschen's
dowry. As bearing indirectly yet forcibly upon a
general consideration of the cases of these young
men, the statement may be added that one of them
had made for his proposed father-in-law several excellent pairs of shoes, while the other had made for
—or, rather, against—him only a series of uncom-
monly sharp bargains.

To neither of the lovers did Andreas give an immediate answer. He must think a little, he said.
The self-esteem of the Herr Strauss was a trifle ruffled by the suggestion that in such a case waiting of
any sort was necessary ; it seemed to him that an offer so desirable as that which he had made was entitled to instant acceptance. But Ludwig noted a
certain trembling in the voice that bade him wait,
and was not so completely engrossed with his own
hopes of happiness but that he could perceive its
cause and could feel sorrow for it. All these years
had Andreas cared for this sweet Roschen, and had
cherished her as his dearest treasure ; and now, when
the best time of her life had come, he was asked to
give her up to a love that rested its claim for recognition upon nothing more substantial than promises
of care - taking which the future might or might
not make good. That Andreas, under such circumstances, even should consider his request, touched
Ludwig's good heart with gratitude ; and the love

that he had for a long while felt towards the old man led him now to put an arm around his shoulder, as a son might have done, and to tell him that the home which he had ready for Roschen was ready for Roschen's father too. And Ludwig's voice also trembled a little. Andreas did not speak, but he put his thin hand into the big brown hand—much stained with the dark wax which shoemakers use and with long handling of leather—that Ludwig held out to him; and when they had stood together thus affectionately for a little time they parted, silently.

In truth, Andreas was more deeply moved than even Ludwig, for all his affectionate sympathy, had divined. His love for Roschen was a double love. With the love of a father he had watched over her these many years; yet even stronger had come to be his love for her as her mother born again. Sometimes, for whole days together, confusing the past with the present, he would call her Christine; and in his heart he ever gave greater room to the fancy that the life which he had hoped for was realized, and that the life which he was living was a dream. No wonder, then, that he asked for a little time in which to school himself to meet the fate that at a single blow brought destruction to his dear home on earth and to his dearer castle in the air.

Roschen was abroad that afternoon, and as Andreas, alone with his birds, turned over in his mind the answers which he must give to these young men —who sought to take to themselves, for the greater pleasure of their young lives, the single happiness

which his old life had left to it—a great bitterness
possessed his soul. When they had so much and he
so little, it was cruel of them to seek to rob him
thus, he thought. And their love, after all, was but
the growth of a day, while his love had been growing steadily for forty years. Roschen was to him
at once the sweetheart of his youth and the dear
daughter of his age. How could these young fellows have the effrontery to place their own light
love fancies in rivalry with this profound love of
his that was rooted in all the years of a lifetime?
His thoughts went back to those long-past days
when he and Christine first had known each other
as little children on the sunny slopes of the Andreasberg, and when began the love that still was a living
reality. And then he followed downward through
the years his own love-story from this its beginning
—the promise made in the twilight, while the south
wind, laden with the sweet smell of the pine-trees of
the Schwarzwald, played about them; the hard parting; his joyous journey with his birds westward
across the sea; the black day when that journey
ended; the years of sorrow which closed in still
keener sorrow when his Christine was lost to him
utterly in death; and then through the later years,
which ever grew brighter and happier as his love
for Christine was born anew and lived its strange,
half-real life in his love for Christine's child, who
also was the daughter given him by Heaven to cheer
and comfort him in his old age. And now at the
end of it all he was asked to give to another this

sweet flower of love that for his happiness, almost
by a miracle, as it seemed, a second time had bloom.
ed.   Was not this asking more of him, he thought,
than rightly should be asked?

So heavy was the load of bitterness that oppress-
ed him that even the singing of the Kronprinz, who
was moved to break forth into song just then, failed
for a time to arouse him.   Yet presently the sweet
sound penetrated the thick substance of his sorrow, and slowly turned the current of his sombre
thoughts.   Andreas loved all music; but because of
the long train of associations which it invoked, and
because of his skilled knowledge of its quality, there
was no music so sweet to him as the singing of a
bird.   And when the singer was the Kronprinz, who
sang with a mellow sweetness rare and wonderful,
the music never failed to move his tender nature to
its very depths.   And so, as he listened to the singing of his bird, gentler and better thoughts possessed him; and then he reproached himself for the
selfishness that had so filled his heart.   He had no
right, he thought, to stand in the way of Roschen's
happiness—to compel her to take the old love that
he had to give in place of the fresh young love that
was offered to her.   It was only a foolish fancy, this
that he had cherished, that she was his sweetheart
of long ago; it was the rational truth that he had to
deal with—that she was his daughter, who had given
him in full measure a daughter's love and duty, and
for whom now, as was a father's duty, he must
secure a good husband, who would care for her

well and loyally when death had taken her father
from her. This was the right conclusion, but all
the strength of his will was required to bring him
to it; and when at last he said to himself that what
so plainly was right should be firmly done, the color
suddenly left his face, and there went through his
heart the sharp pang that he had learned to dread
because of the agony of it. So wrenching was the
pain that he could not repress a cry; but it was not
a loud cry, and the sound of it was lost in the glad
carolling of the Kronprinz's song.

When Roschen came home, a little later, she was
frightened by finding her father looking so pale and
worn; but the sight of her dear face, and her loving
looks and words, revived him quickly, and her fear
passed by. And she forgot her fear the sooner because of the momentous question which he then opened to her; for this last sharp seizure, keener than
any that had preceded it, had warned Andreas that
the duty which he had to do should not be delayed.

Very tenderly and lovingly did he speak of this
heart matter to his little rose, his Roschen, as she
sat beside him on a low stool, after the childish
habit that she never had relinquished, while her
head was nestled against his breast, and while he
stroked her fair hair gently with his thin, delicate
hand. And as he made clear to her all that she
was to know, and explained to her that the decision
between these rival lovers, or the rejection of them
both, must be made by herself, the rosiness of this
pretty Roschen became a deep crimson, and her

head sank down upon her father's breast so that her
face was hid from him; and as his arms clasped her
closely to this loving haven she fell to crying gently
there, as in such cases is a proper maiden's rather
unreasonable way.

"Does the thought of lovers make thee sad, my
little one?" Andreas asked; and he could not quite
stifle, though he tried hard to stifle, the hope that
perhaps Roschen might settle this present matter so
that for a little time longer she still would be wholly
his own.

"It is not the thought of lovers, dear father,"
Roschen answered, and her voice was low and broken, "but the thought that anything should take
me away from thee."

The hope grew larger in the heart of Andreas,
but he said: "The young Herr Strauss will make
thee a fine husband, my daughter. He is a rich
young man already, and—"

But Roschen promptly cut short this eulogy by
raising her head abruptly and saying, with great
decision: "He is a horrid young man, and nothing
is good about him at all. He tries to cheat thee
whenever he comes here to buy our birds; and—
and he has said things to me; and he—and he tried
to kiss me. Ugh! I will have nothing to do with
the Herr Strauss—nothing at all!"

As she spoke, Roschen held up her head firmly
and looked Andreas straight in the eyes. Her own
eyes quite sparkled with anger, for all the tears that
were in them; and the tone in which she pronounced

the name of the Herr Strauss suggested pointedly that he was one of the various unpleasant creatures which humanity disposes of with tongs. All this was so emphatic that Andreas suffered his hope to grow yet stronger; for now, certainly, one of these lovers was put safely out of his way.

"And Ludwig, my little one?"

Roschen did not speak, but the angry sparkle that was in her eyes gave place to a softer and much pleasanter brightness, and a still deeper crimson showed in the pretty face that she hid again suddenly upon her father's breast.

"And Ludwig?" Andreas repeated.

But still Roschen did not speak. She put her arms around her father's neck, and nestled her head beneath his chin in a lovingly coaxing way that she had devised when she was a little child; and then she fell again to sobbing gently.

"Hast thou, then, nothing to say of this friend of ours, my daughter?" Andreas spoke eagerly, his hope being very strong within him now; for he was not versed in the ways of maidens, and the silence that would have been so eloquent to another woman or to a wiser man conveyed a very false notion to his mind.

"Thou hast told me, dear father, that Ludwig makes very good shoes," Roschen said at last, speaking hesitatingly, and in a voice so low that it was little more than a whisper.

"Yes," Andreas answered, somewhat taken aback by the irrelevant and very matter-of-fact nature of this remark; "yes, Ludwig makes good shoes."

"And thou likest those which he has made for thee?"

"Truly. They are good shoes. They have cured my corns." Andreas spoke with feeling. He was sincerely grateful to Ludwig for having cured his corns. "But it is not of Ludwig's shoes that we are talking now, my Roschen," he went on. "It is of Ludwig himself. Hast thou nothing to say in answer to what he asks?"

Through her tears Roschen laughed a little, and she pressed her head still more closely beneath her father's chin. "Thou dear foolish one," she said, "canst thou not understand?" And then, after a moment of silence, she went on: "Hast thou not seen, dear father, how all the birds love Ludwig, and of their own accord go to him?"

Then a little light broke in upon Andreas, and the hope that he had cherished began to pale; but he answered stoutly: "Yes, the birds love him, for he is a good young man. And thou, my daughter?"

And Roschen answered in a voice so low and tremulous that Andreas divined rather than heard the words she spoke: "Perhaps it is with me also, dear father, as it is with the birds!"

For a little time there was silence—for Andreas did not trust himself to speak while his hope was dying in his heart—then he raised the pretty head from its resting-place upon his breast, and as he kissed the forehead that was so like the dead Christine's,

"'*Perhaps it is with me also, dear father, as it is with the birds.*'"

he said, reverently and tenderly : "For thy good and happiness, my dear one, may God's will be done." And as he clasped her again to him closely, the Kronprinz once more lifted up his voice in sweetest song.

When at last Roschen raised her rosy, happy face from her father's breast, she was so full of the wonder that had come to pass that she did not perceive his weary look, nor how pale he was ; yet less pale now than a little time before when his face was unseen by her.

And presently the rosiness of this sweet Roschen grew still deeper as the shop door opened, with a great tinkling of its little bell, and Ludwig entered. Andreas arose from his chair slowly—but neither of them noticed how feeble and labored were his motions, like those of a weak old man—and clasped in both of his own Ludwig's great brown hand, while with a look of love he said: "It is as thou wouldst have it, my son. This dear rose of my growing will bloom in thy garden now "—and he led Ludwig to where Roschen, who indeed was a true rose just then, was standing and put her hand in his.

And then, with a wistful eagerness, he went on: "And thou wilt care for her very tenderly and well, in my place? Thou canst not understand what my love has been ; part of it, I know, has been foolishness—and that which thou wilt give her, if it be strong and steadfast, will be far better than ever was mine. For it is the way of life "—and here the voice of Andreas trembled and fell a little—"that for young hearts love also must be young."

"With God's help, dear father, I will be true and good to her," Ludwig answered, speaking with a stout heartiness that gave the ring of truth to his words; "and I will care well for her and for thee too."

"For me it will not be long," Andreas answered; "but give the care which thou wouldst have given to me to these my birds."

"Do not make us sad to-day, dear father, by such gloomy words," said Roschen, as she put her arms around his neck. "To-day a beautiful time of happiness has begun for us."

"Truly a beautiful time of happiness has begun," Andreas answered; "and I thank God that I have seen its beginning—for when grief comes to thee, and grief must come to us all, my daughter, thou hast now a strong young heart to stay and comfort thee. Yes, this is truly the beginning of a happy time." It was with a very tender smile that Andreas spoke these cheery words; and he added, cheerily: "Now go out into the Square, my children, and say to each other the words which I know are in your hearts. I will be glad in your happiness as I sit here among my birds."

And so Andreas, for the second time in his life, was left alone with his birds.

As he sat there, desolate, he buried his face in his hands, and between his thin fingers there was a glistening of tears. It was so hard to bear! They might have waited just a little while, he thought; it would not have been very long. For he forgot, and perhaps it would be unfair to blame him for forgetting, his own desire that before that little time should pass his Roschen should have assured to her the good care-taker whom she surely would need when the season of sorrow came. A little thrill of pain, a premonition of which he knew the meaning, ran through him.

Then it was that the Kronprinz began to sing. The notes at first were low and liquid, and they fell soothingly upon the ears, and so into the heart of this poor Andreas; and as they rose higher and fuller and clearer, light began to show for him where only darkness had been. The other birds, fired to emulation by these mellow warblings, joined in a sweet chorus, above which the strong rich notes of the Kronprinz rose in triumphant waves of harmony. And gladness came then into the heart of Andreas, and great thankfulness; for as the music of the birds exalted him he seemed to see with a strange clearness into the depths of the future, and all that he saw there promised well for those whom he loved. Such wonderful music was this that the very air about him seemed to be growing goldenly radiant; and with a certain awe creeping into his heart he seemed to hear low echoes of a music even more ravishingly beautiful that came faintly yet with a bell-like clearness from very far away.

Truly there was something strange about this music, for even Bielfrak, who was grown to be a deaf,

17

rheumatic old dog now, heard it and was greatly moved by it. From his comfortable rug in the corner he raised himself painfully upon his haunches, and, pointing his noise upward, uttered a long melancholy howl. Then he came by slow effort across the room to where his master sat and laid his head upon his master's knee. And there was a puzzled look upon Bielfrak's face, for never before had he thus manifested the love that was in his honest heart without finding a quick response to it in the gentle touch of his master's hand. Yet now that hand remained most strangely still, and it was strangely white, and Bielfrak drew back suddenly from touching it—finding it most strangely cold.

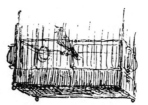

The birds had been frightened into silence by Bielfrak's howl, but now they all burst forth again into the song of strange and wonderful sweetness that of a sudden they had learned to sing. In waves of harmony the chorus rose and fell, and above all sounded the notes of the Kronprinz, rich, full, clear, so delicately perfect as to seem a blending of sunlight and of sound. And in this song there was a strain that seemed to tell of restful triumph and eternal joy. And on the gentle, kindly face of Andreas, as he sat there so very quietly while all the air around him with these sweet sounds was vibrant, there was a most tender smile that told of perfect peace.

THE END.